JENNIE ADAMS

Invitation to the Prince's Palace

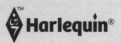
™
Harlequin®

TORONTO NEW YORK LONDON
AMSTERDAM PARIS SYDNEY HAMBURG
STOCKHOLM ATHENS TOKYO MILAN MADRID
PRAGUE WARSAW BUDAPEST AUCKLAND

Recycling programs
for this product may
not exist in your area.

ISBN-13: 978-0-373-17822-3

INVITATION TO THE PRINCE'S PALACE

First North American Publication 2012

www.Harlequin.com

Printed in U.S.A.

Australian author **Jennie Adams** grew up in a rambling farmhouse surrounded by books, and by people who loved reading them. She decided at a young age to be a writer, but it took many years and a lot of scenic detours before she sat down to pen her first romance novel. Jennie has worked in a number of careers and voluntary positions, including transcription typist and preschool assistant. She is the proud mother of three fabulous adult children, and makes her home in a small inland city in New South Wales. In her leisure time Jennie loves long, rambling walks, discovering new music, starting knitting projects that she rarely finishes, chatting with friends, trips to the movies and new dining experiences.

Jennie loves to hear from her readers, and can be contacted via her website at www.jennieadams.net.

Books by Jennie Adams

HIS PLAIN-JANE CINDERELLA
SURPRISE: OUTBACK PROPOSAL
WHAT'S A HOUSEKEEPER TO DO?
DAYCARE MOM TO WIFE

Other titles by this author available in ebook format.

For Kara

CHAPTER ONE

'YOU'RE here. I expected to have to wait longer.' Melanie Watson tried not to sound too desperately relieved to see the cab driver, but she *was* relieved. She'd been saving money to try to start a new life away from her aunt, uncle and cousin. She still didn't have enough, but tonight she'd experienced very clearly just how soul-destroying it truly could be to live among people who postured rather than accepted, who used rather than loved.

The family's gloves had come off and Mel had made the choice to leave now whether she was quite financially ready, or not.

Mel had waited until her cousin had disappeared into her suite of rooms, and until her aunt and uncle had fallen into bed. She'd cleaned up every speck of the kitchen because she never left a job half done, and then she'd ordered a cab, left a note in her room, packed her life into suitcases and carried it to the kerb.

Mel tried to focus her gaze on a suburb painted in shades of silvery dawn. The sun would rise fully soon. The wispy chill would lift. Clarity and the new day would come and things would look better. If she could only stay awake and alert for that long.

She really felt quite odd right now, off kilter with an unpleasant buzzing in her head. She didn't exactly feel she might be about to faint, but…she didn't feel right, that was for sure.

'It's a nice time for a drive. It'll be really quiet and peaceful.' That sounded hopeful, didn't it? At least a little bit positive and not overly blurry?

With the kind of anonymity born of speaking to a total stranger, Mel confided, 'I'm a bit under the weather. I had an allergic reaction earlier and I didn't get to take anything for it until just now. The medication is having a lot stronger impact on me than I thought it would.'

She'd got the treatment from her cousin's stash while Nicolette had seen off the last of the wealthy guests. Maybe Mel shouldn't have helped herself that way, but she'd been desperate.

Mel drew a breath and tried for a chirpy tone that emerged with an edge of exhaustion. 'But I'm ready to leave. Melbourne airport here we come.'

'I arrived earlier than anticipated so I'm grateful that you are ready.'

She thought he might have murmured, 'Grateful and somewhat surprised' before he went on.

'And I'm pleased to hear your enthusiasm despite the problem of allergies. Might I ask what caused them?' The taxi driver's brows lifted as though he didn't quite know what to make of her.

Fair enough. *Mel* didn't know what to make of herself right now. She'd fulfilled her obligations, had pulled off all the beautiful desserts and other food for the dinner party despite harassment from her relatives and cleaned up afterwards when the party had finally ended.

Now she really needed her wits about her to leave, and they weren't co-operating. Instead, they wanted to fall asleep standing up. Like a tram commuter after a big day's work, or a girl who'd taken a maximum dose allergy pill on top of a night of no sleep and wheezing and swallowing back sneezes and getting a puffy face and puffy eyes.

'My cousin bought a new perfume. She sprayed it near me and off I went. Apparently I'm allergic to gardenias.' Mel dug for the remnants of her sense of humour. She knew it was still in there somewhere! 'Just don't give me any big bunches of those and I'm sure we'll be fine.'

'I will see to that. And you are right. It is a good time for a drive. The Melbourne cityscape is charming, even in pre-dawn light.' His words seemed so serious, and his gaze focused on her eyes, then on the spot where the dimple had come and gone in her cheek as she made her small joke. Would the dimple have offset her red nose and puffy face? Somehow Mel doubted it.

Mel focused on him, too. It was difficult not to because the man was top-to-toe gorgeous. Tall, a little over six feet to her five feet four and beautifully lean. Mel blinked to try to clear her drowsy vision.

He'd spoken in that lovely accent, too. French? No, but something European, Mel thought, to go with his tanned skin and black hair and the almost regal way he carried himself. He had lovely shoulders, just broad enough that a woman could run her hands over them to appreciate their beauty, or lay her head to rest there and know she could feel secure.

He wore an understated, expensive-looking suit. That was a bit unusual for a cab service, wasn't it? And his eyes—they weren't hazel or brown but a glorious deep blue.

'I just want to curl up.' Maybe that explained her reaction to him because his broad shoulders looked more appealing by the moment.

'Perhaps we'd better get your luggage loaded first, Nicol—' The rest of the word was drowned by the double beep of a car's unlocking device. He reached for the first two suitcases.

She must have given her full name of Nicole Melanie Watson when she booked the taxi. Since going to live with her aunt and uncle at age eight, Mel had only been known by her middle name. It felt strange to hear the first one again. Strange and a little shivery, because, even hearing only part of the word, his accent and the beautiful cadence of his voice made it sound special.

Oh, Mel. For goodness' sake.

'It's a pretty set of luggage. I like the floral design.' Was *Mel* making sense? She'd rescued the luggage when her cousin Nicolette had wanted to throw it out, but of course this man didn't need to hear that. And *she* didn't need to be quite so aware of him, either!

'You wouldn't lose the luggage easily. The design is

quite distinctive.' He cast her a sideways glance. 'You are quite decided about this?'

'I'm decided.' Had he had people try to scam him out of fares? Mel would never do that. She knew what it was like to try to live on a tight budget. Her aunt and uncle might be well off, but they'd never seen the need to do more than meet the basic costs of taking her in. Once she reached working age, they'd expected her to return their investment by providing cheap kitchen labour. For the sake of her emotional health, Mel had to consider any debt paid now. 'I won't change my mind.'

She glanced to where he'd parked and saw, rather than a taxicab, an unmarked car. The cab agency had said there was a shortage of cabs but she hadn't realised someone might come for her in their private car in their off-duty time. Wouldn't that be against company policy?

And the car was a really posh one, all sleek dark lines and perfectly polished. That didn't seem right for a cab driver, did it? How would he afford it? Mel frowned.

'Did you come straight from a formal dinner or something?' It must have been a really late night.

The words slipped out before she could censor them. The thought that followed worried her a little, but he'd have had sleep wouldn't he? He looked rested.

You'll be perfectly safe with him, Mel. It won't be like—

She cut the thought off. That was a whole other cause of pain for Mel, and she didn't want to let it in. The night had been tough enough.

'Most dinners I attend are formal unless I have a night with my brothers.' Rikardo spoke decisively and yet…his guest didn't look as he'd expected. She didn't…*seem* as he'd expected. Her openness and almost a sense of naivety…must be because she wasn't feeling well.

He tucked the odd thoughts away, and tucked his passenger into the front seat beside his. 'You may rest, if you wish. Perhaps by the time we arrive at the airport your allergy medication will have done its job and you'll be back to normal.'

'I doubt that. I feel as though I've been felled by elephant medicine.' She yawned again. 'Excuse me. I can't seem to stop.'

He'd collected a drowsy and puffy version of Sleeping Beauty. That was what Prince Rikardo Eduard Ettonbierre thought as the airport formalities ended and he carried Nicolette Watson onto the royal private jet and lowered her into a seat.

She'd slept most of the way to the airport and right through the boarding process. The medication had indeed got the better of her, but she was still very definitely…a sleeping beauty.

Despite the puffy face she seemed to have held her age well since the days when she'd been part of his university crowd during his time in Australia. She'd been two years behind him, but he'd known even then that Nicolette wanted to climb to the heights of social success.

Though their paths had not crossed since those days,

Nicolette had made it a point to send Christmas cards, mark his birthday, invite him as her personal guest to various events, and in other ways to keep her name in front of him. Rik had felt awkward about that pursuit. He didn't really know what to say now, to explain his lack of response to all those overtures.

Perhaps it was better to leave that alone and focus on what they were about to achieve. He'd carefully considered several women for this task. In the end he'd chosen to ask Nicolette. He'd known there would be no chance he would fall for her romantically, and because of her ambitious nature he'd been confident she would agree to the plan. She'd been the sensible choice.

Rik had been right about Nicolette. When he'd contacted her, she'd jumped at this opportunity to elevate her social status. And rather than someone closer by, who might continue to brush constantly through his social circles once this was all over, when their agreement ended, Rik could return Nicolette to Australia.

'You should have allowed me to carry her, Your Highness.' One of his bodyguards murmured the words not quite in chastisement, but in something close to it. 'Even driving a car by yourself to get her— You haven't given us sufficient information about this journey to allow us to properly provide for your safety.'

'There is nothing further to be revealed just at the moment, Fitz.' Rik would deal with the eruption of public and royal interest in due course but there was no need for that just yet. 'And you know I like to get behind the wheel any time I can. Besides, I let you follow in a second car and park less than a block away.

Try not to worry.' Rik offered a slight smile. 'As for carrying her, wasn't it more important for you to have your hands free in case of an emergency?'

The man grimaced before he conceded. 'You are correct, Prince Rikardo.'

'I *am* correct occasionally.' Rik grinned and settled into his seat beside Nicolette.

Was he mad to enter into this kind of arrangement to outwit his father, the king? Rik had enjoyed his combination of hard work and fancy-free social life for the past ten years. As third in line to the throne, he'd seen no reason to change that state of affairs any time soon, if at all. But now…

There were deeper reasons than that for your reluctance. Your parents' marriage…

His bodyguard moved away, and Rik pushed that thought away, too. He wasn't crazy. He was taking action. On these thoughts Rik turned his attention to the sleeping woman. Her hair fell in a soft honey-blonde curtain. Though her face still showed the ravages of her allergy problem, her features were appealing.

Long thick brown eyelashes covered eyes that he knew were a warm brown colour. She had soft pink lips, a slim straight nose and pretty rounded cheeks. She looked younger in the flesh than in the photo she'd emailed, than Rik had thought she would look now…

She sighed and Rik had an unexpected urge to gently kiss her. It was a strange reaction to what was, in the end, a business arrangement with a woman he'd never have chosen to know more than peripherally if not for this. A response perhaps brought on because she seemed vulnerable right now. When she woke from this sleep she would be once again nothing but the ladder-climbing socialite he'd approached, and this momentary consciousness would be gone.

The pilot commenced take-off. Rik's guest stirred, fought for a moment to wake. Her hand rose to her cheek.

'You may sleep, Nicolette. Soon enough we will take the next step.' He said it in his native Braston tongue, and frowned again as the low words emerged. He rarely spoke in anything but French or English, unless to one of the older villagers or palace staff.

Nicolette turned her head into the seat. Her lashes stopped fluttering and she sighed. She'd cut her hair too, since the emailed photo she'd sent him. The shoulder-length cut went well with the flattering feminine skirt and silk top she wore with a short cardigan tied in a knot at her waist. The clothing would be nowhere near warm enough for their arrival in Braston, but that would be taken care of.

Rik made his chair comfortable, did the same for his sleeping guest, and took his rest while he could find it. When Nicolette sighed again in her sleep and her head came to rest on his shoulder, Rik shifted to make sure she was comfortable, inhaled the soft scent of a light, citrus perfume, and put down the feeling of contentment to knowing he was soon to take a step to get his country's economy back on its feet, and outwit his father, King Georgio, at the same time. Put like that, why wouldn't Rik feel content?

* * *

'You had an uneventful flight, I hope, Your Highness?'

'Not too much longer and we'll be able to disembark, Prince Rikardo.'

Mel woke to voices, snippets of conversation in English and another language and the low, lovely tones of her taxi driver responding regally while something soft and light and beautifully warm was draped around her shoulders.

'What—?' Heart pounding, she sat up abruptly.

This wasn't a commercial flight.

There were no rows of passengers, just some very well-dressed attendants who all seemed to make her taxi driver the centre of attention in a revering kind of way.

Mel's allergy was gone. The effects of the medication had worn off. That was good, but it also meant she couldn't be hallucinating right now.

She had vague memories of sleeping…on an accommodating shoulder.

Yet she didn't remember even boarding a flight!

This plane was luxurious. It had landed somewhere. Outside it was dark rather than the sunshiny day she'd looked forward to in Melbourne, and Mel could feel freezing air coming in through the aperture where another attendant waited for a set of steps to be wheeled to the edge of the plane.

She should be feeling Sydney summer air.

Memory of that expensive-looking car rose. Had she been kidnapped? Tension coiled in her tummy. If anything was wrong, she'd left a note saying she was moving to Sydney. Her relatives might be angry to lose their underpaid cook, but she doubted that they would go looking for her. Not at the expense of their time or resources.

Breathe, Melanie. Pull yourself together and think about this.

The driver had asked her if she was 'sure about this'. As though they already had an arrangement? That would make it unlikely that she'd been kidnapped.

But they *didn't* have an arrangement!

Mel turned her head sharply, and looked straight into the stunning gaze of the man who'd placed her in that car.

She'd thought, earlier, that he was attractive. Now Mel realised he was also a man of presence and charisma. All those around him seemed to almost feel as though…they were his servants?

Words filtered through to Mel again. French words and, among those words, 'Prince Rikardo'.

They were addressing her driver as a prince?

That was easy, then, Mel thought a little hysterically. She'd fallen down a rabbit hole into some kind of alternative world. Any moment now she would sprout sparkling red shoes. *That's two different fairy tales, Mel. Actually it's a fairy tale and a classic movie.* Oh, as though that mattered! Yet in this moment, this particular rabbit hole felt all too real. And maybe there'd been a book first, anyway.

Stop it!

'You're fully refreshed? How are the allergies? You slept almost twenty-four hours. I hope the rest helped you.'

Did kidnappers sound calm, rational and solicitous?

Mel drew a breath, said shakily and with an edge of uncertainty she couldn't entirely hide, 'I feel a bit exhausted. The allergies are gone. I guess I slept them off while we travelled between Melbourne and…?'

'Braston.' He spoke the word with a slight dip of his head.

'Right. Yes. Braston.' A small country planted deep in the heart of Europe. Mel had heard of it. She didn't really know anything about it. She certainly shouldn't *be anywhere near it.* 'I'm just not quite sure— You see, I thought I'd be flying from Melbourne to Sydney—'

'We were able to fly very directly.' He leaned towards her and surprised her by taking her hand. 'You don't need to be nervous or concerned. Just stick to what we've agreed and let me do the talking around my father, the king.'

'K-king.' As in, a king who was the father of a prince? As in, this man, Rikardo, *was* a prince? A royal prince of Braston?

Stick with the issue at hand, Mel. Why are you here? That's the question you need answered.

'You are different somehow to what I have remembered.' His words were thoughtful.

'Remembered from our drive to the airport? I don't understand.' Her words should have emerged in a strong tone. Instead they were a nervous croak drowned by the clatter of a baggage trolley being wheeled closer to the plane.

Well, this was *not* the time for Mel to impersonate a scaredy frog waiting to be kissed into reassurance by a handsome prince.

Will you stop with the fairy-tale metaphors already, Melanie!

'You're nervous. I understand. I'll walk you through this process. Just rely on me, and it will be easy for both of us to honour our agreement.'

Mel drew a deep breath. 'Seriously, about this "agreement". There's been—'

'Your Highness, if you and your guest would please come this way.' An attendant waved them forward.

The prince, Rikardo, took Mel's elbow, tucked the wonderful warm wrap more snugly about her shoulders, and escorted her to the steps and down them onto the tarmac.

Icy wind whipped at Mel's hair and stung her face but, inside the wrap, she remained warm. Floodlights lit the small, private airstrip. A retinue of people waited just off the tarmac.

Mel had an overwhelming urge to turn around and climb back onto the plane. She might not be down a rabbit hole, but she was definitely Alice in Crazyland. None of this would have happened if she'd been completely herself when she ordered that ride to the airport and believed it had arrived. Mel would never take someone else's medication again, even if it were just an over-the-counter one that anyone could buy!

'Please. Prince…Your Highness…' As she spoke they moved further along the tarmac. 'There truly has been some kind of mistake.'

What could have happened? As Mel asked the silent question puzzle pieces started to come together.

If he'd called at the right address, then he had expected to collect a woman from there.

Her cousin had been in a strange mood, filled with secrecy and frenetic energy. At the end of the dinner party, Nicolette had rushed to her room and started rummaging around in there. Had Nicolette been…packing for a trip?

Rik had said he'd arrived earlier than he'd expected to. That would explain Nicolette not being ready. Mel had thought that he'd called her by her first name of Nicole, but it could have easily been 'Nicolette' that he said. She and her cousin looked heaps alike. Horror started to dawn. 'It must have been Nicolette—'

'Allow me to welcome you on to Braston soil, Nicolette.' Rikardo, *Prince Rikardo*, spoke at the same time. He stopped. 'Excuse me?'

Oh. My. God.

He'd mistaken Mel for Nicolette. Mel's *cousin* had made some kind of plan with this man. That meant Rikardo really was a prince. Of this country! As in, royalty who had made an arrangement with Nicolette.

Mel, the girl who'd worked in her aunt and uncle's kitchen for years, was standing here in a foreign country with an heir to the throne, when it was her cousin who should be here for whatever reasons she should be here. How could the prince not realise the mistake? Surely he'd have seen that Mel wasn't Nicolette, even in dawn light and with Mel affected by allergies? Just how well did this prince know Nicolette?

Yes, Mel? And how many times has Nicolette become

furious when one of her acquaintances mistook you for her when they called at the house?

'Unless we're in the public eye, please just call me Rik.' He hustled her into the rear of another waiting car and climbed in beside her. A man in a dark suit climbed into the front, spoke a few words to the prince in French, and set the vehicle in motion.

The prince added, 'Or Rikardo.'

'You probably have five given names and are heir to a whole lot of different dukedoms or things like that.' Mel sucked up a breath. 'I do watch the news and see the royal families coming and going.' She just hadn't seen this particular royal. 'The most famous ones. What I mean is, I'm not an overt royal-watcher, but I'm also not completely uninformed.'

Which made her sound like some kind of overawed hick who wouldn't have a clue how to behave in such august company. Exactly what Mel was! 'Please… Prince…Rik…I need to speak to you. It's urgent!'

'We have arrived, Your Highness.' The words, spoken in careful English, came again from the driver.

He'd drawn the car to a whisper-quiet halt and now held the door open for them to alight. Rikardo would get out first, of course, because he was, after all, a prince.

A burst of something a little too close to hysteria rose inside Mel's breast.

'Thank you, Artor, and also for speaking in English for the benefit of our guest.' Rikardo helped Mel from the car. He glanced down into her face. 'I know you may be nervous but once we get inside I will take you to our suite of rooms and you can relax and not feel so pressured.'

'S-straight to the rooms? We won't see anyone?' Well, of course they would see people. They were seeing people right now. And what did he mean by *their* suite? 'Can we talk when we get there? Please!'

'Yes, we will talk. It shouldn't be necessary at this late stage, but we will discuss whatever is concerning you.' He seemed every inch the royal as he said this, and rather forbidding.

Mel's stomach sank even further. She hadn't meant for this to happen. She hadn't meant to do anything other than take a taxi to the airport. She had to hope it would be relatively easy to fix the mistake that had been made.

Rik whisked her up an awe-inspiring set of steps that led to a pair of equally stunning studded doors. As they approached the doors were thrown open, as though someone had been watching from within.

They would have been, wouldn't they? Mel glanced up, and up again, and still couldn't see the ending of the outside of this enormous palace. Parts of it were lit, other parts melted into the surrounding darkness. It looked as though it had been birthed here at the dawn of time. Mel shivered as the cold began to register, and then Prince Rik's hand was at her back to propel her the final steps forward and inside.

Voices welcomed their prince. Members of the royal retinue of staff stood to attention while others stepped forward to take the prince's coat, and Mel's wrap.

How silly to feel as though the small of her back

physically held the imprint of the prince's fingers. Yet if he hadn't been supporting her Mel might have fainted from the combination of anxiety and feeling overwhelmed by the opulence.

The area they entered was large, reaching up three levels with ornate cornicing and inlaid life-sized portraits of royal family members fixed into the walls. A bronze statue stood to one side on a raised dais. Creams and gold and red filled the foyer with warm resplendence. It would be real gold worth more than an entire jewellery store.

'Welcome to the palace.' Rik leaned closer to speak quietly into Mel's ear.

'Thank you. That is…' Mel's breath caught in her throat as she became suddenly very aware of his closeness.

She'd laid her head on his shoulder, had slept the hours of the flight away inhaling the scent of his cologne. On some level of consciousness, Mel knew the pace of his breathing, knew how it felt to have him sleep with his ear tucked against the top of her head. The feel of the cloth of his suit coat against her arm, his body warmth reaching her through the fabric.

For a moment consciousness and subconscious memory, nearness and scent and whatever else it was that had made her aware of him even initially through a fog of medication, filled Mel. She forgot the vital need to explain to him that he'd made a mistake and she had, too. She forgot everything but his nearness, and the uneven beat of her heart.

And then Prince Rikardo of Braston spoke again, softly, for her ears only.

'Thank you for agreeing to help me fulfil my father's demands and yet maintain my freedom…by temporarily marrying me.'

CHAPTER TWO

'THERE'S been a terrible mistake.' Rik's bride-to-be paced the sitting room of his personal suite. Tension edged her words. One hand gestured. 'I don't belong here. I'm not the right girl. Look at all this, and I'm—'

'You won't be staying here all that long.' Not for ever. A few months… Rik tried to understand her unease. She'd been fully willing to enter into this arrangement. Why suffer a bout of cold feet about it now? She'd stepped into his suite, taken one glance around and had launched into speech.

'This is an interlude,' he said, 'nothing more.' And one they'd agreed upon, even if she hadn't yet signed the official contract. Rik's aide had the paperwork in a safe place, but it was ready and waiting, and Nicolette had made it clear that she was, too. So what had changed?

She drew a shuddery breath. 'This is gilt and gold and deep red velvet drapes and priceless original artworks and cornices in enormous entryways that take my breath away. This is more than a rabbit hole and a golden pumpkin coach and a few other fables meshed together. This is—' Her brown-eyed gaze locked with his and she said hotly as though it were the basis of evil: *'You're a prince!'*

'My royal status is no surprise to you.' What did surprise Rik was how attractive he found the sparkle in her eyes as indignation warred with guilt and concern on her lovely face. He'd never responded this way to Nicolette. He didn't want to now. This was a business arrangement. His lack of attraction to Nicolette was one of the reasons he'd chosen her. It would be easy to end their marriage and walk away.

So no more thoughts such as those about her, Rik!

'But it is a surprise. I mean, it wouldn't be if I'd already read about you in a magazine or something and I certainly completely believe you.' Shaking fingers tucked her hair behind her ear.

She didn't even sound like the woman he remembered. She sounded more concerned somehow, and almost a little naïve.

A frown started on his brow. He'd put down her openness, the blurting of a secret or two to him when he collected her, to the influence of the allergy medication. But that had worn off now. Suspicion, a sense of something not right, formed deep in his gut. He took a step towards her, studied her face more closely and wished he had taken more notice of Nicolette's features years ago. Those freckles on her nose—? 'Why do you seem different?'

'Because I'm not who you think I am,' she blurted, and drew a sharp breath. Silence reigned for a few seconds as she seemed to gather herself together and then she squared her shoulders. 'My full name is *Nicole Melanie* Watson.'

'Nicole...'

'Yes.' She rushed on. 'I'm known as Melanie and have been since I went to live with my aunt, uncle, and cousin *Nicolette* when I was eight years old. *Nicolette* would fit right in here. I've tried to figure this out since I woke up in your private jet and realised I wasn't at Sydney airport about to get off a plane there and go find a hostel to stay in while I searched for work because I could no longer stay—'

She broke off abruptly.

Sydney airport? Hostel? Search for work? There was something else about her statement, too, but Rik lost the thought as he focused on the most immediate concerns.

'I am not certain I understand you.' His tone as he delivered this statement was formal—his way of throwing up his guard. 'Are you trying to tell me—?'

'I think you meant to collect Nicolette and you got me by mistake. I don't see what else could have happened. When you said my name before, I thought you said Nicole, not Nicolette. I thought I must have given my full name when I ordered the taxi.'

'If what you say is correct...' Rik's eyes narrowed. Could this be true? That he'd collected the wrong woman? 'I haven't seen Nicolette for a number of years, just a photo sent over the Internet. I thought when I collected you that you'd changed and that you looked younger than expected. If you are not Nicolette at all— Do you look a great deal like your cousin?' He rapped out the words.

'Y-yes, at least a fair amount. And I sound like her. It really annoys her. Acquaintances do it all the time when they come to the house. Mistake us for each other, I mean.' The woman—Melanie—wrung her hands together. 'This is all just a horrible mix-up. I was zonked out on medication, and waiting at the kerb for my ride to the airport to start a whole new life and you took me instead of taking Nicolette, who probably should have been waiting but she's never on time for anything, and you said you were early.'

Horror came over her face. 'Nicolette will be *furious* at me when she finds out what's happened.'

'It is not up to your cousin to take out any negative feelings on you if a mistake has been made.' A thought occurred to him. 'While I thought you were your cousin, you…mistook me for a taxi service?'

'I didn't know then that you were a *prince*!'

Did his lips twitch? She sounded so horrified, and Rik had to admit the idea of being mistaken for a cab driver was rather unique. His amusement faded, however, as the seriousness of the problem returned to the forefront of his thoughts. He didn't notice the way his face eased into gentleness as he briefly touched her arm.

'I'm sure there'll be a solution to this problem.' He bent his thoughts to coming up with that solution. He had planned all this, worked everything out. And after a long flight to get to Australia from Braston…he'd collected a cousin he'd never heard of, who had no idea of his marriage plans, the bargain Rik had struck with his father, King Georgio, or the ways in which Rik intended to adhere to that bargain but very much on his terms.

If he couldn't straighten this all out, his error could cost him the whole plan, and that in turn could cost the people of Braston who truly needed help. Rik held himself substantially responsible for that need.

'It's kind of you not to want to blame me.' She spoke the words in a low, quiet tone and gazed almost with an edge of disbelief at him through a screen of thick dark lashes.

As though she didn't expect to be given a fair hearing, or she expected to be blamed for what had happened whether she was in the wrong or not.

'There's no reason to blame you, Nicol—*Melanie*.' For some reason, Rik couldn't shift his gaze from the surprised and thoughtful expression in her eyes.

She looked as though she didn't quite feel safe here. Or did she always carry that edge of self-protectiveness, that air of not knowing if she was entirely welcomed and if she could let down her guard?

Rik had lived much of his life with his guard firmly in place. As a royal, that was a part of his life. But he knew who he was, where he fitted in the world. This young woman looked as though she should be happy and carefree. She had said she'd been about to start a new life. What had happened to make her come to that decision? To leave her family at dawn with all her suitcases packed?

Had Nicolette contributed to that sudden exit on Melanie's part?

You have other matters to sort out that are of more immediate concern.

Rik did, but he still felt protective of this young woman. She'd suddenly found herself on the other side of the world in a strange place. A little curiosity towards her was to be expected, too. He'd collected a stranger. Naturally he would want to understand just who this stranger was.

He would need her help and co-operation to resolve this problem, and she would need his reassurance. 'This doesn't have to be an insurmountable difficulty. If I can get you back out of the palace, keep you away from my father and create a suitable story to explain that bringing my fiancée home took two trips...'

'It seems such a strange thing to do in the first place, to marry someone for a brief period knowing you're going to end the marriage. Why do it at all if that's the case? How well do you know my cousin?' The words burst out of Mel as she watched Prince Rikardo come to terms with the problem of a girl who shouldn't be here, and one who should be and wasn't.

She felt overwrought and stressed out. What would happen to her plans now? Mel needed to be in Sydney looking for work. Not here suffering from a case of mistaken identity.

And then she realised that she'd just questioned a prince, and perhaps not all that nicely because she *did* feel worried and uneasy and just a little bit threatened and scared about the future. 'I beg your pardon. I didn't mean that to sound disrespectful. I guess I'm just looking for answers.'

'Your cousin is a past acquaintance from my university days in Australia who has kept in touch now and then remotely over the years since.'

So he didn't know Nicolette closely, had potentially never really known her. But he'd said he intended to marry her, albeit briefly. Mel's mind boggled at the potential reasons for that. Nicolette had hugged the secret close. Maybe she'd been told she had to? What was in it for Mel's cousin?

Well, even if it were to be a brief marriage, Nicolette would for ever be able to say she'd been a princess. Mel's cousin would love that. It would open even more doors socially to her. That left what was in it for Prince Rikardo?

'This must all seem quite strange to you, to suddenly find yourself here when you thought you were headed for Sydney, wasn't it?' His voice deepened. 'To start a new life?'

'I did say that, didn't I? When I thought you were a taxi driver and blabbed half my life story at you.' She drew a breath. 'I also meant no insult by thinking that you were a taxi driver.'

'None was taken.' He paused.

Did he notice that she dodged his question about starting a new life? Mel didn't want to go into that.

'Let me get the wheels in motion to start rectifying this situation,' he said. 'Then we'll discuss how this happened.'

For a blink of time as he spoke those words Mel saw pure royalty. Privileged, powerful. He would not only fix this problem, he would also have his answers.

He'd said he didn't blame her, that it wasn't her fault. But Mel couldn't be as self-forgiving. She should have realised something was amiss. There'd been signs. An unmarked car; a driver not in uniform; even the fact that he'd tucked her in the front of the cab beside him rather than expecting her to get in the back. Of course he would demand his answers. Had she really thought she would get off without having to face that side of it?

Would she in turn learn more of why he'd chosen her cousin for this interaction? 'Yes, of course you'll need to set wheels in motion, to contact Nicolette and sort out how to get her here as quickly as possible. I'm more than willing to simply be sent to Sydney. You can put me on any flight, I don't mind. I don't need to see my cousin again.' She didn't *want* to see Nicolette again and be brought to account for all of this, and for choosing to leave the family without a moment's notice, because Mel *wouldn't* go back.

What did Prince Rikardo see in Nicolette?

He didn't have to see anything.

Or maybe he liked what little he knew of Mel's cousin and they could conduct this transaction between them and perhaps even become firm friends afterwards. Nicolette could be charming when it suited her. There'd been times over the years when she'd charmed Mel. Not lately, though.

Mel searched Rikardo's gaze once more. Though his mind must be racing, he didn't appear at all unnerved. How could he portray such an aura of strength? Did it come as part of his training in the royal family? An odd little shiver went down her spine and her breath caught.

What would it be like, to be a prince such as Rikardo Ettonbierre? Or to be…truly in Nicolette's shoes, about to marry him, even if briefly?

Are you sure that his strength is simply a result of his position, his royal status, Melanie?

No. There was something in Rikardo Ettonbierre's make-up that would have demanded those answers regardless, and got them whether he'd ever been trained to his heritage, or not. That would have shown strength, not uncertainty, no matter what.

'We will make all the necessary arrangements. If we do it quickly—' Rikardo strode towards a phone handset on an ornate side table. He lifted the phone and spoke into it. 'Please ask my aide to attend me in my suite as soon as possible. I have some work for him to do. Thank you.' He had just replaced the receiver when a knock sounded on the door.

'That's too soon to be my aide,' he murmured. 'It will be our dinner. You must be hungry.'

The door opened. Members of staff entered bearing covered dishes. Aromas filled the room and made Mel realise just how long it had been since she'd eaten.

'The food smells delicious.' She'd always *cooked* the meals, not had them brought to her on silver salvers. 'I have to confess I *am* quite hungry.'

'That is good to hear.'

Rather than from Rikardo, the words came in a more mature yet equally commanding voice. The owner of that voice stepped into the room, a man in his early sixties with black hair greying at the temples, deep blue eyes and the power, by his presence alone, to strike dumb every staff member in the room.

Mel hadn't even needed that impact to identify him, nor the similarities to the prince. All she'd needed was one look at Rikardo's face, at the way it closed up into a careful mask that covered and protected every thought.

The king had just walked in.

This was the worst thing that could have happened right now. They'd needed to keep her, Melanie, out of sight of this man. Mel's breath froze in her throat and her gaze flew to Rik's. What did they do now? She caught a flash of a trapped look on Rikardo's face before he smoothed it away.

Somehow that glimpse of humanness opened up a wealth of fellow feeling in Mel. She had to help Rik out of this dilemma. She didn't even realise that she'd thought of him as Rik, not Rikardo.

The king's gaze fixed on her, examining, studying. He'd spoken to her. Sort of. Mel didn't know whether or not to respond.

'Indeed, Father, and it is fortuitous that you are here.' Rik stepped forward. He didn't block his father's view of Mel, but he drew the king's attention away from her. 'I would like a word with you regarding the truffle harvest, if you please.'

The older man's eyes narrowed. He frowned in his son's direction and said: 'It *pleases me* to know my future daughter-in-law will eat a meal rather than pretend a lack of appetite to try to maintain a waif-thin figure.'

Waif-thin figure?

Mel worked in a kitchen. She might have been underpaid, but she'd never been hungry. Was it usual for kings to speak their minds like this?

There was another problem, though. Even Mel, with her lack of understanding of royal protocols, could guess that it wasn't appropriate for Rikardo not to introduce her to his father, even if the king had surprised them in Rik's suite.

Should she introduce herself? Why hadn't Rikardo done that?

Because you're not who you should be, Melanie. How is he supposed to introduce you without either telling the truth or lying? Neither option will work just at the moment.

And anyway, why don't you interview all the kings you're on a first-name basis with, and collate the responses to discover a mean average and then you'll know whether they all speak bluntly?

She wasn't thinking hysterically exactly, Mel told herself.

Just don't say anything. Well, not anything bad. Be really, really careful about what you say, or, better still, stay completely silent and hope that Rikardo takes care of this. Didn't he say earlier if you came across his father to let Rik do all the talking?

Yes, but that was before he realised Mel wasn't Nicolette. His father didn't know that, though, and now the king had spotted Melanie. Not only spotted her but spoken to her and had a really good look at her. And if she didn't respond soon, the king might think—

'Your Highness.' Mel sank into what she hoped was an acceptable style of curtsy. She tried not to catch the older man's gaze, and hoped that her voice might pass for Nicolette's next time.

Rikardo had mistaken Melanie for Nicolette. But she'd been puffed up with allergies then. Rikardo strode towards the door of his suite.

At the door, he turned to face Mel. 'If you will excuse us? Please go ahead and eat dinner.' He asked one of the kitchen staff to let his aide know they would speak after Rikardo finished with the king. From outside, Rikardo called in another member of staff. 'Please also show my guest her rooms.'

In about another minute, the king would be out of here. Mel could stop holding her breath and worrying about what she might reveal to the king that could cause problems for when Nicolette arrived.

Mel glanced into Rikardo's eyes and nodded, acknowledging that he intended to leave.

Rikardo swept out of the room and swept his father along with him, even if he was the king.

Melanie thanked the staff for the delivery of the meal. She felt their curious gazes on her, too, and she would have liked to strike up a conversation, to ask what it was like to work in the kitchens of a palace. Instead, she kept her gaze downcast and kept the interaction as brief as she could.

The rooms she would use were lavish. Mel could barely take it all in.

And then finally she was alone.

So she could sit at the royal dining table in Prince Rikardo's suite that had its own guest suite within it, and eat royal food while she waited for the prince to have his discussion with his father about truffle harvesting. She hadn't known the country grew truffles.

But that wouldn't be all of the conversation and it would no doubt be difficult for the prince, but then Rikardo would come back here and tell Melanie his plans, and somehow or other it would all be all right.

Mel turned to the dining table, looked at the array of dishes. She would eat so at least she had some energy inside her to deal with whatever came next.

It *would* be all right. Rikardo was a prince. He would be able to make anything right.

CHAPTER THREE

RIK stood by the window in the sitting area of his suite. Early sunlight filtered across the snowy landscape of mountains and valleys, and over Ettonbierre village below. Soon people would begin to move around, to go about their work—those who *had* enough work.

He had once liked this time best of all, the solitude before the day's commitments took over. Today, his thoughts were already embroiled and his aide already on his way to Rik's suite to discuss yet another matter of urgency. The past two years had been problem after problem. Rik's marriage plans had been part of the solution, or so he had believed. Now...

He had spoken to his father last night. It hadn't been the greatest conversation he'd ever had; it had taken too long, and at the end of it he had known the impossibility of trying to bring Nicolette out here now to pass her off as his fiancée.

Really he'd known that from the moment Melanie had told him he'd collected the wrong girl. Too many people had seen her. Then Rik's *father* had seen her. She had tried not to be too noticeable, too recognisable. But the king *had* noticed. Right down to the three freckles dotted across the bridge of her nose.

Rik had whisked his father out of his suite. He'd bought a little time to come up with a solution before his father formally met his fiancée. But in the end there *was* only one solution.

A soft knock sounded on the outer door of his suite. Rik strode towards it. He didn't believe in the edict that a prince should not do such menial things as open doors to his staff. He and his brothers all worked on behalf of the people of Braston one way or another, so why wouldn't they open a door?

And now you all have a challenge to fulfil. The prize is that your father will come out of his two-year disconnection from the world around him, caused by the queen moving out and refusing to return, and co-operate to enable the economy here to be healed.

'Good morning, Prince Rikardo.' His aide stepped into the room and closed the door behind him. 'My apologies for disturbing you at this hour.'

'And mine for disturbing you late last night.' Rik gave a wry twist of his lips. 'To examine an emailed photograph, no less.'

And the passport of Nicole Melanie, which had been handled by one of his retinue of attendants when they arrived at the airport with his guest deeply asleep.

Nicole, not Nicolette. Only Rik could have spotted that mistake and he'd been otherwise occupied at the time.

'But with a purpose, Your Highness. It is unfortunate that the two women do not look enough alike to ensure we could safely swap them.' Dominico Rhueldt drew a breath. 'I have carried out your wishes and transferred the funds from your personal holdings to the bank account of Nicolette Watson, and ordered the set from the hand-crafted collection of the diamond jeweller, Luchino Montichelli. It will be delivered to Nicolette within two days.'

The man hesitated. 'Your Highness, I am concerned about the amount of money going out of your holdings towards relief to the people. I know they are in need—'

'And while I have the ability I will go on meeting needs, but that doesn't fix the underlying problems.' Rik sighed. It was an old conversation. 'Nicolette. She is happy with this...buy-off?'

A gift of baubles and a cash injection in exchange for her acceptance of the changed circumstances, and her silence.

Though Rik's question referred to the woman he'd organised to briefly marry, he struggled to shift his thoughts from the one he'd carried onto a plane recently.

He glanced at the closed door of his guest suite. Last night when he'd got back, he'd tucked the covers over Melanie. She'd been curled up on the bed in a ball as though not quite sure she had a right to be there. Sleeping Beauty waiting to be woken by a kiss.

The nonsense thoughts had come to him last night. A result of tiredness and the suppression of stress, Rik had concluded. Yet the vision of her curled up there was still with him. The desire to taste softly parted lips, still there. He'd been absorbed in Braston's problems lately. Perhaps it had been too long since he took care of those other needs.

His aide rubbed a hand across the back of his neck. When he spoke again, his words were in French, not English. 'Nicolette acknowledged the payment and the order of the diamond jewellery as her due as a result of the changed circumstances. She accepts the situation but it is good, I think, that she will be unaware of any other plans you may intend to implement until such time—'

'Yes.' If 'such time' was something Rik could bring about.

'The other matter of urgency,' his aide went on, 'is unfortunately, the truffle crop.'

Rik swung about from where he'd been half gazing out of the windows. One search of Dominico's face and Rik stepped forward. 'Tell me.'

'Winnow is concerned about the soil in one of the grove areas. He feels it looks as it did last year before the blight struck again.'

'He's tested it? What is the result? We were certain we'd prevented any possibility of this happening this year. The crop is almost ready for harvest!' Rik rapped the words out as he strode to his suite. He stepped into the walk-in closet and selected work wear. Khaki trousers, thick shirt and sweater, and well-worn work boots. A very un-princely outfit that his mother would have criticised had she been here to do so. Rik started to shuck clothes so he could don the new ones.

His aide spoke from a few feet away. 'Winnow is doing the testing now.'

'I will examine the soil myself and speak with Winnow.' Rik laced his boots and strode into the sitting room.

'Your guest?' Dominico also glanced towards the closed door of the guest suite. 'Shall I wake her? Inform her of your immediate plans?'

'Allow her to sleep on while she has the chance. She had a long and difficult day before we arrived here. Please ask, though, that Rufusina be prepared to go with me to the groves.'

Melanie heard these words faintly through a closed door. She shifted in the luxurious bed, opened her eyes to a canopied pelmet draped above her head, and remembered curling up for just a moment while she waited for Prince Rikardo to return from speaking with his father. Now she was under the covers. Still in her clothes, but as though someone had covered her up to make sure she'd be comfortable. And that was Rik's voice out there, and it sounded as though he was about to go out.

Who was Rufusina?

'I'm getting up.' The words emerged in a hoarse croak. She cleared her throat, sat up, and quickly climbed out of bed. And called more loudly. 'Prince— Your Highness—I'm awake. I'm sorry I fell asleep before you got back last night. I'll be out in five minutes. I won't keep you waiting.'

Only after she called the words did Mel realise how they might have sounded to members of staff if any were out there with him, and, given he'd just spoken to someone, they probably were.

Heat rushed into her face, and then she felt doubly silly because she hadn't meant the words in that way, and the staff wouldn't care anyway, surely. And Rikardo would send her back to Australia today so none of this would be her problem for much longer.

Mel stopped in her headlong dash to the bathroom and wondered where the burst of disappointment had come from.

From being in a real live palace for a night and having to go home now, she told herself. And perhaps just the tiniest bit because she wouldn't have the chance to get to know Rikardo better.

'That's *Prince* Rikardo to you, Melanie Watson, and why would he want to get to know you? You're a cook. Not even a formally qualified one. You're not even in his realm.' She whispered the words and quickly set about putting herself together so she wouldn't keep the prince waiting.

Well, she *was* in his realm—literally right now. But in terms of having anything in common, she didn't exactly fit here, did she? No doubt he would want to speak to her sooner, rather than later, to tell her how he would get rid of her and how soon Nicolette would arrive to make everything as it was supposed to be.

That would be fine. Mel would co-operate fully. She only wanted to be sent home so she could get on with her life! Preferably avoiding contact with Nicolette in the process.

Outside in the sitting area, Rik's gaze caught with his aide's. 'I cannot be in two places at once right now. It would be rude to abandon Melanie now that she is awake, but breakfast must be offered, and I need to get to the groves.'

'Permit me to suggest a picnic breakfast for you and your guest after you have attended the groves. It would be easily enough arranged.' Dominico, too, glanced at the closed door of the guest suite. 'You might have a nice, quiet place in mind?'

Rik named a favourite place. 'That would be convenient to speak to Melanie there and see if she can find her way clear—'

'I hope I didn't keep you waiting.' The guest in question pushed her suite door open and stepped into Rik's sitting room.

Rik's head turned.

His aide's head turned.

There were appropriate words to be uttered to help her to feel comfortable, to extend grace. Rik wanted to do these things, to offer these things, but for a moment the words stuck to the back of his tongue as he gazed upon the morning face of Melanie Watson.

Soft natural colour tinged her cheeks. She'd tied her hair back in some kind of half-twisted ponytail. Straight falls escaped to frame the sides of her face. She wore a long, layered brown corduroy skirt trimmed in gold, brown ankle boots with a short heel and rubber-soled tread, and a cream cashmere sweater. In her hands she held a wool-lined coat. Her lips bore a soft pink gloss and she'd darkened her lashes with a touch of mascara.

Her clothing was department or chain store, not designer. The hairstyle had not come at the expense of an exclusive salon or stylist but thanks to a single brown hair tie and a twist of her hands. Yet in those five minutes she had produced a result that had knocked Rik out of his comfort zone, an achievement some had striven for and failed to achieve, in various ways, in decades of his life.

'You look lovely.' The inadequate words passed across his lips. A thought quickly followed that startled him into momentary silence. He wanted his brothers to meet her.

Maybe they would, if either of them were around today. And maybe Melanie would be on her way back to Australia before any chance of such a meeting could occur.

He stepped forward, lifted her right hand in his, and softly brushed her fingers with his lips. 'I hope you slept well and feel rested.' He introduced his aide. 'Dominico assists me with all my personal and many of my business dealings.'

In other words, his aide could be trusted utterly and was completely aware of their situation. At the moment, Dominico was more aware than Melanie.

Rik truly did need to speak with her, to set all matters straight as quickly as possible. He hoped that Melanie might co-operate to help him but it was a great deal to ask.

So much for your arrogant belief that you could outwit your father, still get all that you want, and not have to pay any price for it aside from the presence of a fiancée here for a few months.

Rik had collected the wrong woman and created a lot of trouble for himself.

So why did he feel distracted by the feel of soft skin against his lips? Why did he wish that he could get to know Melanie?

He pushed the thoughts aside. There was work to do. A truffle crop to bring to fruition disease-free, and a woman to take to breakfast. 'Will you join me for a walk outdoors? I need to attend to some business and then I thought we might share a picnic breakfast. I know a spot that will be sheltered from wind and will catch the morning sunshine. We can speak privately and I can let you know the outcome of my discussion last night with my father.'

'A—a picnic breakfast would be lovely, but is it all right for people to see me?' Her balance wobbled just enough to make him think she might have been about to curtsy to him. 'I'm sorry I wasn't still awake when you finished speaking with your father last night. It would have been okay to wake me up. I must have crawled under the covers.'

She hadn't. Rik had tucked her in. Had paused to gaze at a face that seemed far too beautiful. He suspected it had occurred to her that he might have tucked her in. The flush in her face had deepened.

Rik realised he still had hold of her hand. He released it and stepped back. 'It will indeed be fine. You are dressed well for the conditions. Shall we?'

Rikardo led Melanie through corridors and along passageways and past vast rooms with domed ceilings. Everywhere, staff worked with silent efficiency, going about their day's tasks.

Without making it seem a big deal, he explained

that she never needed to curtsy to anyone but his father or mother, and to them only in certain formal circumstances.

'Am I likely to meet your mother this morning?' Mel glanced about her and tried not to let an added dose of apprehension rise.

Rikardo shook his head. 'No. The queen is away from the palace.'

'Well, thank goodness for that, anyway,' she blurted, and then grimaced.

But Rikardo merely murmured, 'Indeed,' and they fell silent.

In that silence, Melanie tried not to let her mind boggle at the thought that she was walking through a palace beside a prince, and feeling relieved not to be about to meet a queen, but it all did feel quite surreal. Rikardo nodded to a staff member here or there. He'd said it was fine to be seen out with him by anyone they came across, so Mel would take that at face value. He'd obviously come up with some explanation for her presence.

'The kitchens here would be amazing.' She almost whispered the words, but she could imagine how many staff might work there. The amazing meals they would prepare. Mel felt certain the royal staff wouldn't have cake plates thrown at their heads as her cousin had done to her that final night.

Rikardo turned to glance at her. 'You can see the kitchens later if you wish.'

Before she left for the airport. Mel reminded herself deliberately of this.

'I didn't know that Braston grew truffles. I probably should have known.' She drew a breath. 'I've never cooked with them. My relatives loved throwing dinner parties but they were too—'

She bit the words back. She'd been going to say 'too stingy' to feed their guests truffles.

'Truffles have been referred to as the diamonds of the kitchen. Along with tourism they have represented the main two industries for Braston for some years now.' Rik stepped forward and a man in liveried uniform opened the vast doors of the palace and suddenly they were outside in the morning sun with the most amazing vista unfolding all around.

'Oh!' Melanie's breath caught in her throat. Everywhere she looked there were snow-capped mountains on the horizon. A beautiful gilded landscape dotted with trees, hills and valleys and sprinkled with snow spread before them. 'I didn't see any of this last night. Your country is very beautiful. I'm sure tourists would love to see it, too.'

'It is beautiful, if small.' Pride found its way into Rikardo's voice. 'But much of Europe is, and there are countries with more to offer to travellers. I would like to see an improvement in the tourist industry. If my brother Anrai has his way that will also happen very soon.'

Melanie liked his pride. Somehow that seemed exactly as it should be. And also the warmth in his tone as he referred to a brother. That hadn't been there when he'd spoken about the king or the queen, and, even if she'd only met the king briefly and had tried not to catch his attention too much, Georgio did seem to be a combination of forthrightly spoken and austere that could strike a girl as quite formidable.

You could handle him. If you managed yourself among your aunt and uncle and cousin for that many years and held onto your sense of self worth, you can do anything.

It hadn't hurt that Mel had set up a back-door arrangement and sent lots of cakes and desserts and meals out to a local charity kitchen to be shared among the masses. Her relatives never had caught on to that, and Mel had had the pleasure of giving away her cooking efforts to people who truly appreciated them.

Well, that life was over with now. Over the past year or so the family had forgotten to give her the kind moments that had balanced the rest. They had focused on the negative, and Mel had started saving to leave them. Now she just had to get back to Australia and to Sydney so she could start afresh.

It would be all right. She'd get work and be able to support herself. It didn't matter if she started out with very little. She pushed aside fears that she might not be able to find work before her meagre savings ran out.

Instead, she turned to smile at Rikardo. He looked different out of doors and in profile in these surroundings, more rugged somehow.

Face it, Mel. He looks attractive no matter what light you see him in, and each new light seems to make you feel that he's more attractive than the last one. And that moment of shared consciousness when she first stepped into his sitting room this morning. Had she imagined that?

Of course she'd imagined it. Why would a prince be conscious of…a kitchen hand? *A cook.* Same difference. They were both worlds away from being an heir to a kingdom.

'We commercially grow black truffles here.' Rikardo spoke in a calm tone. 'If you are not aware of it, truffles have a symbiotic relationship with the roots of the trees they grow under.'

'In this case oak trees,' Melanie murmured while she tried to pull her thoughts together. *Was* he calm? If so, his threshold for dealing with problems must be quite high. 'That's what they are, isn't it?'

Her glance shifted below them to the left where grove upon grove of trees stood in carefully tended rows. 'I'd heard that truffles could be grown commercially in that way. I think in Tasmania—'

'That's correct, and, yes, they are indeed oak trees.' He'd taken her arm, and now walked with her towards a grouping of …

Outbuildings? Was that a fine enough word for buildings within the palace grounds? There were garages with cars in them. Sports cars and other cars. Half a dozen at least. They all looked highly polished and valuable. They would go very fast.

Did the sun go in for just a moment? Mel turned her glance away. A man drove past them in one of the vehicles. Rik raised an arm as the driver slowed and tooted the horn before driving on. 'That is Anrai.'

'I thought he resembled you in looks.' Except Rikardo was far more handsome. And having her arm held by him made Mel way too conscious of him.

Small talk, Mel. You're supposed to be indulging in polite, get-to-know-you-but-don't-be-nosy-about-it small talk. 'How many brothers do you have?'

'Just the two, both older than me and busy trying to achieve their own plans—' He broke off.

A worker walked towards them, leading…a pig with a studded red collar around its neck. When the animal saw Rikardo, it snorted and almost pulled the worker over in its enthusiasm to get to the prince.

Rikardo looked down at the animal and then turned to Mel. 'This is Rufusina. She is a truffle hog and will be coming to the groves with us this morning.'

'*This* is Rufusina?' For some reason Melanie had pictured a gorgeous woman in an ankle-length fur-lined coat with long flowing brown hair. Maybe the woman had known Rikardo for ever and had secretly wanted to marry him herself.

Can we say overactive imagination? Well, this was the perfect setting for an imagination to run wild in! Mel tried to refocus her thoughts. 'She's a very interesting-looking truffle hog. She looks very…'

Porcine?

'Very intelligent,' Mel concluded.

'I am sure that is the first thought that comes to all minds.' For the second time since they'd met, Rikardo's lips twitched. Though his words laughed at Mel just a little, they laughed at Rufusina, too, for there was a twinkle in his eye as he watched the hog strain at her leash to get to him, and succeed.

Rikardo then told the hog to 'sit' just as you would say to a dog. The pig planted her haunches and cast an adoring if rather beady gaze up at him. She got a scratch behind each ear for her trouble. Rikardo took the lead.

They were at the groves before Mel had come to terms with her prince having a pet pig, because, whether he'd said so or not, this animal had been raised to his hand.

Mel would guarantee it. She could *tell*. They arrived also before Mel could recover from the beauty of Rikardo's twinkling eyes and that hint of a smile.

And what did Mel mean by '*her* prince' anyway? He certainly wasn't! She might have him for a few more hours, if that, and all of which only by default anyway because she'd been silly enough to think he was a cab driver.

Later, after she'd been returned to Australia, she could write her story and send it in to one of those truth magazines and say she'd spent a few hours with a royal.

She wouldn't, of course. She wouldn't violate Rikardo's privacy in that manner.

Today, in the broad light of Rikardo's…kingdom, Mel couldn't imagine how she'd mistaken him for anything other than what he was, whether she'd been overtired and overwrought and under the influence of an allergy medication or not.

It wasn't until they reached the actual truffle groves that Mel started to register that Rikardo seemed to have somehow withdrawn into himself as they drew closer to his destination. She wasn't sure how to explain the difference. He still had her arm. The pig still trotted obediently at his side on its lead. Rikardo spoke with each person they passed and his words were pleasant, if brief.

But Rikardo's gaze had shifted to those rows of oak trees again and again, and somehow Mel *felt* the tension rising within him as they drew nearer.

'Winnow.' Rik greeted a spindly man in his fifties and shook his hand. 'Allow me to introduce my guest, Miss Watson.'

So that was how Rik planned to get around that one. But would that be enough? Because for all the people that mistook Mel for her cousin, plenty more…didn't.

'Do you have the results of the soil test, Winnow? Are we infected again with the blight?'

This time Mel didn't have to try to hear the concern in Rikardo's tone.

'The test shows nothing, Prince Rik.' The man stopped and glanced at Melanie and then back to the prince. 'I beg your pardon. I mean, Prince Rikardo.'

'It's fine, Winnow. We are all friends here.' Rik dipped his head. 'Please go on.'

Winnow pulled the cap from his head and twisted it in his hands. 'The test shows nothing, but last year and the year before…'

'By the time the tests showed positive, it was too late and we ended up losing the crop.'

'Yes. Exactly.' Winnow's face drew into a grimace. 'I cannot prove anything. Maybe I am worrying unduly but the soil samples that I pulled this morning do not *look right* to me.'

'Then we will treat again now.' Rikardo didn't hesitate. 'Yes, it is expensive and a further treatment we hadn't planned for will add to that expense, but our research and tests show that enough of the treatment will

keep the blight at bay. If you have any concern whatever, then I want the treatment repeated.'

The older man blew out a breath. 'I am sorry for the
added expense but my bones tell me—'

'And we will listen.' Rikardo clapped the man on
the back. 'Order the treatment. I will draw funds for it.'

From there Rikardo examined the soil samples himself, and took Rufusina into one of the groves to sniff
about. Mel didn't fully understand the process. The
older Winnow kept lapsing into the beautiful local
dialect as he spoke with Rikardo.

It was worth not being able to understand, to hear
Rikardo respond at times in kind. She felt as though
she'd heard him speak to her in the same language but
she must have imagined that. In any case it was very
lovely, a melodious harmony of tones and textures.

'We will take breakfast up there, if you are agree-
able.' Rikardo pointed to a spot partway up a nearby
mountainside. He'd handed the truffle hog over to
Winnow, who was about to put her to good use in the
groves before seeing her returned to her home. And
with an admonishment to ensure the pig didn't run off,
as she was apparently wont to do on occasion.

But right now…

There was a natural shelving of rock up high where
a bench seat and table had been set into it. The view
would be amazing. 'Oh. That would be lovely.'

They began the climb. 'The truffles. Will they be
okay?'

'I hope so. We've had two years of failed harvests.
That has resulted in a devastating financial blow to the

country's economy while we searched for a preventative treatment that would work without affecting the quality of the truffles.' He led her to the bench seat and table.

Opposite was a mountain with large sections covered in ice. Mel sat, and her glance went outward and down, over groves of trees and over the village named after the royal family. 'There must be so much rich history here. I'm sorry that there have been difficulties with the truffle industry. From Winnow I gather you play a key role in this truffle work?'

'I run the operations from ground level to the marketing strategies.'

Mel's gaze shifted to the village below. 'You must care about the people of Braston very much.'

'I do, and they are suffering. Not just here and in Ettonbierre village, but right across the country.' He drew a breath. 'I had planned that we should eat while I led up to my request but perhaps it is best to simply state it now and then explain.'

Mel's breath locked in her throat. Rikardo had a request of her? She glanced again at the scene below. Rikardo led a privileged life compared to the very ordinary ones playing out down there. There was a parallel to her life with Nicolette and her cousin's parents. But there was also a difference.

Rikardo seemed willing to go to any lengths to help those who depended on his family for their livelihoods. 'What can I do to help you? To help…them?'

'You are kind, aren't you?' It wasn't a question, and he seemed as concerned by it as he was possibly admiring of it. 'Even though you don't know what I may want.'

Mel lowered her gaze. 'I try to be. What is it that you need?'

'If it is at all possible, if it's something you can do without it interfering unreasonably with your life or plans and I can convince you that you will be secure and looked after throughout the process and after it, I would like to ask you to take Nicolette's place.' Blue eyes fixed on her face, searched.

'T-take her place?' She stuttered the question slightly.

If Mel had peered in front of her in that moment, she felt quite certain she would have seen a hole. A rabbit hole. The kind that Alice in Crazyland could fall down.

Or leap into voluntarily?

'Just to be clear,' Mel said carefully, 'are you asking *me* to be the one to temporarily marry you?'

CHAPTER FOUR

'I KNOW a marriage proposal must seem quite strange when you expected to be sent back to Australia today.' Rik searched Melanie's face.

He felt an interest and curiosity towards her that he struggled to explain.

And an attraction that can only get in the way of your goals.

He couldn't let that happen. And right now he needed to properly explain his situation to her. That meant swallowing his pride to a degree, something he wasn't used to doing. Yet as he looked at the carefully calm face, the hands clenched together in the folds of her skirt as she braced herself for whatever might come next, it somehow became a little easier.

At worst she would refuse to help him.

That would be a genuine 'worst', Rik. You need her help, otherwise you'll end up locked into a miserable marriage like that of your parents, or unable to help the people of Braston at all because this plan of yours has failed.

'May I be plain, Melanie?'

'I think that would be best.' She drew an uneven breath. 'I feel a little out of my depth right now.'

She would feel more so as he explained his situation to her. He had to hope that she would listen with an open mind.

'The arrangement that I made,' he said carefully, 'was to bring your cousin over here and marry her a month later.'

Melanie responded with equal care. 'You indicated that would be a temporary thing?'

'Yes.' He sought the right words. 'The marriage was to end with a separation after three months and Nicolette would then have been returned to Australia and a quick divorce would have been filed for.'

'I see.' She drew a breath and her lovely brown eyes focused on his blue ones and searched. 'You didn't intend to let your father know those circumstances until after the marriage, I'm guessing? What did you hope to gain from that plan?'

'Aside from my brothers, Nicolette, and my aide, no one was to know of the plan.' He'd intended to outplay his father, to get what he wanted for the people without having to yield up his freedom for it. 'This plan probably sounds cold to you.'

'It does rather reject the concept of marriage and for ever.' Melanie sat forward on the bench seating and turned further to face him. Her knee briefly grazed his leg as she settled herself.

The colour whipped into her cheeks by the cold air around them deepened slightly. That…knowledge of him, that awareness that seemed to zing between her body and his even when both of them had so much else on their minds...

Is something that cannot be allowed to continue, Rik, particularly if she is willing to agree to the business arrangement you're asking for with her.

'In my family, many lifelong marriages have been made to form alliances or for business reasons.' He hesitated, uncertain how to explain his deep aversion to the idea of pursuing such a path. 'That doesn't always result in a pleasant relationship.'

Melanie's gaze searched his. 'It could be quite difficult for children of such a marriage, too.'

'It's not that.' The words came quickly, full of assurance and belief as though he needed to say it in case he *couldn't* fully believe it?

Rik had his reasons for his decision. He was tired of butting heads with his father while the king tried to bully him to get whatever he wanted. His father needed to acknowledge that Rik would make his own decisions. That was all. 'There have been myriad problems in the past couple of years.

'The first year the truffle crop failed it was difficult.' People relied on the truffle industry for their survival. 'Around that same time, my mother, the queen, moved out. That was an unprecedented act from a woman who'd always advocated practical marriages and putting on a good front to the public, no matter what.'

Melanie covered her surprise. 'That must have caused some complications.'

'It did. For once my father found himself on the back foot.'

'And you and your brothers found yourselves without a mother in residence. I'm sorry to hear that. It's never pleasant when you lose someone, even if they choose to leave.' A glimpse of something longstanding, deep and painful flashed through her eyes before she seemed to blink it away. 'I hope that you still get to see her?'

'I see my mother infrequently when there are royal occasions that bring us all together.' Would Mel understand if he explained that his contact with his mother hadn't changed much? That the queen had never spent much time with her sons and what time she had spent had been invested in criticising their clothing, deportment, efforts or choices in life? Better to just leave that alone.

'My parents died years ago.' She offered the confidence softly. 'I went to live with Nicolette and my aunt and uncle after that happened.'

He took one of her hands into his. 'I'm sorry for your loss.'

Dominico had informed him of some of these things this morning after the security check the aide ordered on her came through. The invasion of Melanie's privacy had been necessary, but Rik had refused to read the report, asking only to be told 'anything that might matter'. Though he had to protect himself, somehow it had still felt wrong.

'Thank you.' She gently withdrew her hand, and folded both of them together in her lap.

She went on. 'You've explained about the truffle crops failing, how that's impacted on your people. One year is a problem but two years in a row—'

'Brought financial disaster to many of our truffle workers.' And while Rik pursued every avenue to find a cure for the blight to the truffle crops, his father had denied the depths of the problem because he was absorbed in his anger and frustration over his queen walking out on him.

'On top of these issues, the tourist industry also waned as other parts of Europe became more popular as vacation destinations. Tourism is Anrai's field. He has the chain of hotels and the country certainly still gets a tourist market, but when there is so much more to do and see just over the border...'

'You have to have something either comparable, or totally unique, to pull in a large slice of the tourist market.' Melanie nodded her head.

'Exactly. Our country needs to get back on its feet. My brothers and I have fought to get our father to listen to the depth of the problems.' They'd provided emergency assistance to the people out of their own pockets as best they could but that wasn't a long-term solution. None of them had endless supplies of funds.

In terms of available cash, nor did the royal estate. It had what it had. History, a beautiful palace and the means to maintain it and maintain a lifestyle comparable to it for the royal family. Their father oversaw all of that, and did not divulge the details of what came and went through the royal coffers. It was through careful investment of a shared inheritance that Rik and his brothers had decent funds of their own.

'Despite these difficulties you came up with a plan.' Mel searched Rikardo's face. Her heart had stopped pounding in the aftermath of his remarkable request, though even now she still couldn't fully comprehend it, couldn't really allow herself to consider it as any kind of reality.

It was Alice down that alternative universe hole again, yet it wasn't. He truly wanted her to marry him. For practical purposes, to outwit his father, and just for a few months, but still…he wanted her to marry him.

She started to find it hard to breathe again. 'And somehow your plan involved trading off a brief marriage for sorting out the country's economic troubles.'

'Yes. My father has pushed all three of us to marry. I think we all have expected that Marcelo would have to do that whether he wanted to or not because he is the eldest. It is part of his heritage.'

Mel nodded. 'I thought when I came here, well, I guess I was so overwhelmed by it all that I didn't stop to think that everything might not be rosy just because there's a palace filled with amazing things. Just because you're a prince doesn't mean everything is easy for you. Or for your brothers, either.'

'My brothers and I went to our father in a concerted bid to get him to listen to the seriousness of the problems the people are facing and with our plans for addressing those problems. Leadership reform is also desperately needed, and that is something Marcelo has been working to achieve for some years now.' Rikardo drew a breath. 'Our father finally did listen. We got our concessions from him.'

His tone became even more formal as he went on. 'But that agreement came at a cost. In return for agreeing to requests that will help us protect Braston's people from further financial hardship, his demand was that we each marry within the next six months.'

'To ensure that the family carries on?' Mel asked the question and then wondered if she should have.

Even as a king, did Georgio have the right to push his sons to marry if they didn't feel ready? If they didn't want to? For Rik to go to such lengths to avoid the institution, he must have some deep-seated reasons. Or did he just not want to be bullied? That was reason enough, of course!

Mel might not ever fully understand, and for some reason she felt a little sad right now. Her gaze shifted to the cliff face opposite. Two men were near the top, tourists or locals with rappelling equipment.

Mel had to navigate *this* discussion. And Rik's explanations did help her to start to understand what was at stake, at least for the people of Braston.

Could she decide to just walk away when the futures of so many people hinged on Rik meeting his father's demands? When him bringing her here by mistake could have ruined those plans? If she hadn't been on the street filled with allergy medication…

Whether she'd meant it or not, her actions had contributed to this current problem, and if there was no other way to fix it…

But it's such a big undertaking, Mel. Marriage, even if it is only for a few months! And there'd be publicity and a dress and so much else, and you'd be fooling Rik's father the whole time and then he'd realise he'd been fooled and be very angry.

Yet Mel knew that Rik would protect her; that he would make sure his father didn't bring any of his wrath down on Mel's head. Rik wouldn't *allow* that anger to have its head. 'When it ended you would send me back to Australia, to Sydney. I wouldn't be exposed to the aftermath here.'

'And because we'd give an interview when we dissolved the marriage and let the magazines and tabloids have that, I would hope you wouldn't attract much media interest when you went home.' His gaze searched hers. 'I would direct them towards me and ask you to do the same. At worst there might be some photographs and speculation about you in the newspapers over there for a brief time.'

That was to be expected when such an event had happened, but if all the information were already given, surely the papers wouldn't care much once they realised Mel wasn't going to talk to them, and the split had been amicable? 'That shouldn't be so bad.' The whole thing wouldn't be too scary if she decided to do it. Would it?

She reached for the picnic basket that sat ignored on the table before them, and hoped that Rik couldn't see the tremble in her fingers. 'Would you like coffee? Something to warm your hands around?'

'Thank you.' His gaze, too, shifted to the men on the nearby mountain peak before it returned to Mel. 'I should have unpacked the basket and made it all available to you the moment we got up here.'

The thought of a prince unpacking breakfast for her horrified her but she bit back her words about it and instead, served the food and coffee for both of them.

When she set his plate in front of him, he caught and held her gaze.

'I know what I'm asking isn't easy. I made this plan because I do not feel I can marry, truly…permanently.' He hesitated. 'The demonstration of that institution within my family—'

'Has been about as warm as what I've seen in Nicolette's family.' Mel bit her lip, but that was her truth and there didn't seem to be much point in avoiding saying it now.

They started on their food. There were eggs cooked similarly to a quiche but without the pastry base. Small chunks of bread dipped in fragrant oil and herbs and then baked until they were crisp and golden. Grilled vegetables and fruits and a selection of pastries.

'What you've asked me to do *is* unexpected.' Stunningly so. 'But I ended up here, you can't swap me for Nicolette, and if I don't agree, the game is up with your father and you either have to marry someone for real and stay married to her, or your father won't grant you the "concessions" you asked for.'

'I'm afraid I didn't allow for collecting the wrong woman outside Nicolette's home, but that is not your fault.' He frowned and sipped his coffee. 'It's important you don't make your decision based on guilt. A mistake happened that was out of my control, and yours.'

She did feel at least partially responsible, but Mel kept that thought to herself and instead took a small bite of a tasty grilled vegetable before she went on. 'I'd like to know what the concessions are that your father has agreed to.'

'I am determined that the truffle crop this year will not fail.' Rikardo set down his knife and fork and turned to face her. 'When it flourishes, I'll need a spectacular marketing idea to get buyers back onside to buy our product. Many of them have lost faith because of the blight that struck our crop two years running.'

Mel, too, set down her utensils. 'What is this marketing idea?'

'On the palace grounds there are truffles that grow naturally.' Rik's gaze shifted to where the palace sat in splendour in the distance. 'For centuries those truffles have been eaten only by royals. It probably sounds rather archaic but—' He shrugged and went on.

'These truffles are particularly fine. If buyers are given the chance to obtain small quantities of them in exchange for purchasing commercial quantities of our regular truffles, I believe they will jump at the opportunity.'

'What a clever idea.' Melanie spoke without hesitation. 'People will go nuts for a chance like that. I can also imagine that you might have had a job on your hands to get the king to allow you to use those truffles.'

'Correct. My father tends to adhere to a lot of the old ways and does not want to consider change.' Georgio was strong, stubborn, unbending. Rik preferred to take the strengths he'd inherited from his father, and turn them to better purpose.

As for Melanie, she looked beautiful and innocent and wary and uncertain all rolled into one as she sat beside Rik on the bench. Yet she also seemed well able to think with a business mind, too, and her eyes shone with genuine encouragement for him as she heard his plans for the truffle marketing.

Would she agree to help him out of the corner he'd got himself stuck in? Did he even have the right to ask that of her?

'I don't want to harm you through this agreement, Melanie.' That, too, had to be said. 'I have asked for your help, but if it is not something you can do, you do not have to give it.'

'But you want to help your people.' Her gaze turned to meet his, and held. 'You chose Nicolette because you weren't...romantically attached to her or anything like that, didn't you?'

'I did. That allowed the situation to remain as uncomplicated as possible.'

'It would be easy to end the marriage and get on with what you really wanted to do with your life afterwards.'

He dipped his head. 'Yes.'

'I'm not ready to consider marriage yet. The real thing, I mean.' Even as Melanie spoke the words, a part deep inside her whispered a question. Did she believe she would ever be ready? Did she even feel she had the right—?

What did she mean by that? Of course she had the right, and she would still have the right if she married Rikardo and they then divorced. Melanie pushed the strange question aside.

And she thought about all those people subject to circumstances beyond their control, just trying to get on with their daily lives. People in a lot of ways who would be just like her. Not royal people, but everyday people who simply needed a bit of a hand up.

Mel could do this. She could be of help. She could make it so Rikardo didn't have to lock himself into a long-term marriage he didn't want. Maybe later he would find someone and be able to be happy. The little prick she felt in her chest must have been hope that he would indeed find that happiness.

'I'll do it.' Melanie spoke the words softly, and said them again more forcefully. 'I'll do it. I'll marry you so you can make your plan work. I want to help you.'

'You're quite certain?' Rik leaned towards her as he spoke.

'I am. I'm totally sure.' And in that moment, Mel was. She could help him. She could do this to make up for him not being able to marry her cousin.

'Thank you, Melanie.'

'You're welcome.' Her face softened and the beginnings of a smile came to her lips. Her gaze moved to *his* lips and suddenly she had to swallow because something told her he was going to kiss her as part of that thank you.

She thought it, and her breath caught, and then he did.

Rik's lips brushed hers in a soft press. His hand cupped her shoulder, and even through layers of cloth Mel felt that. Registered that as she received a kiss from a prince.

That was why it felt so remarkable. It had to be the reason—a kiss from a prince to thank her for agreeing to help him out of a tight corner.

Yet Melanie didn't feel as though a prince was kissing her. She was being kissed…by a man, and it felt wonderful in a way no kiss had before.

In that moment her response was completely beyond her control. Her mouth softened against his, gave itself to his ministrations before her thoughts could catch up or stop her. If those thoughts had surfaced, would the kiss have ended there, with a simple brushing of lips against lips? A simple "thank you" expressed in those terms? Because that was indeed what Rik had set out to do.

It had to have been and yet somehow, for Mel at least, it had become something very different.

Mel closed her eyes. For a moment she forgot she was on a mountainside in Europe with a royal prince, seated at a table with a picnic breakfast spread before them and the most amazing scenic vistas on all sides.

She forgot that it was chilly here but that the sun shone and they were sheltered from the wind. A man was simply kissing her and she was kissing him back and that man had a pet truffle hog he'd named and whom he doted on, even though he tried very hard to hide the fact. He cared for his brothers and for the people who lived in his country, and she'd liked him from the moment she'd thought he was a gorgeous cab driver come to take her away to the airport so she could make her way to Sydney.

'Rik.' She'd slept on his shoulder and blabbed at him when she wasn't quite sensible, and, despite all the smart things she should be thinking right now, the kiss felt right.

'Hmm?' He whispered the half-question against her lips.

Mel didn't know whether she said it, or thought it. She simply knew the words.

Kiss me again.

CHAPTER FIVE

I WOULD kiss you for ever and it would not be enough.

Rik thought the words inside his mind, thought them in his native language. Thought them even though they could not possibly be true and he must simply be swept up in gratitude and relief.

Yet deep within himself he knew that now, in this moment, Melanie would welcome the prolonging of this kiss. His instincts told him this. The way she yielded petal-soft lips to him told him this.

It was that thought of her willingness that finally prompted him to stop something that he should not have started in the first place, and that he hadn't expected would make his heart pound. He, who rarely lost his cool over anything, had been taken by surprise by kissing a slip of a girl up high on a mountainside.

'Thank you...' Rik released Melanie and drew back, and for a moment couldn't think what he was thanking her for.

For rescuing him. The prince was being rescued by the same generosity that he'd felt in Melanie's soft lips.

You are on dangerous ground with this thinking,

Rikardo. If she is kind, then she is kind and that is some-
thing indeed to be appreciated. But the awareness of
each other—that cannot be, and it cannot go on.

He shouldn't have touched her. Arrogantly, he hadn't
known that doing so would be such a stunning thing.

The kiss had been startling in its loveliness. It wasn't
a manly description. But with Melanie it felt exactly
right to describe it in this way.

Melanie was startling in her loveliness, and that
came from the generous way she gave of herself.

He'd meant only to touch her lips with his, should
perhaps not have considered even that much. Rik would
like to say that he'd expected not to feel any attraction
to Melanie, that he had expected to feel as indifferent
towards her as he had felt towards Nicolette, but he'd
known it would be different.

Yet he had kissed her, and had ended up shocked and
a little taken aback by just how much he had enjoyed
that kiss. Her response to him had felt unrehearsed and
open. That, too, had added to her appeal.

Maybe she had simply wanted to kiss a prince.

In many other circumstances, Rik would have accepted the thought and yet Melanie had agreed to help
him for no reason other than out of generosity to try to
help others. She hadn't asked him what she would get
out of the arrangement. She'd wanted to hear the problems and then she'd made a decision based on what she
felt she could do to help.

'I guess we just sealed the bargain.' Her words held
a tremor. She turned to the picnic basket and started
to carefully repack it. 'We should probably get back.

Now that we've made this decision, your father will want that official meeting. That's assuming he can fit me into his schedule. I imagine royal families are very busy and I certainly wouldn't presume—'

'It will be all right, Melanie.' She was fully back into 'dealing with a prince and a promise and a royal family' mode and in feeling out of her depth, though she had valiantly jumped into this for his sake.

And for the sake of the people of Braston.

Did that mean she *hadn't* thought of Rik in that light as they kissed? That he had simply been a man kissing a woman, and she a woman kissing a man? Had his impact on her come completely from Rikardo the man, not from him being the third prince in line to the throne of Braston?

It wasn't a question that should even have mattered. Rik had accepted that women were attracted to his title first, sometimes to the man within, second, but always that first was there.

Perhaps some of his questioning came from the relief of knowing he hadn't blown his chance of avoiding being locked into a miserable marriage as part of his bargain with his father.

Melanie's gaze meshed with his. 'Are *you* quite sure you want to do this? I want to help you and help the people of Braston, but in the end what you do has to be really what you want.'

'I'm sure.' He got to his feet and lifted the picnic basket. 'We may not get much done today other than the meeting with my father if he is available, but Dominico will want to get the ball rolling on a few things.'

Melanie agreed. Now that she had committed to marrying Rikardo, she wanted to get things moving.

She didn't want to stop and give herself too much time to think about the next month and the three that would follow it.

That might have been rather easier for her before they shared that kiss. Mel stumbled slightly on the uneven ground. She didn't want to think about the kiss, either! Her heart still beat hard from its impact.

'I have you.' Rik's hand shot out and grasped her arm.

And I have received the most moving kiss I've ever experienced.

Not that Mel *had* a great deal of experience. Her life with the family had kept her busy. Oh, she'd dated here and there with men that she met out in her 'normal' world. At the fresh produce store, or once it was the delivery guy from the local butcher's shop. There hadn't been a lot of time or opportunity.

There is always the time and the opportunity if you want it enough.

Well, now there was a prince.

No, there wasn't. Not like that. She wasn't dating Prince Rik. She *was* going to marry him, but that was for an agreed purpose that had nothing to do with romance. Right. So she was safe from getting any of the wrong kind of ideas about him or anything like that.

Why then, with Rik's hand on her arm, and the memory of a kiss still fresh in her mind and stamped on her lips, did Mel feel anything *but* safe?

From what? Falling for him? That would be insane.

Much more than falling down a rabbit hole or wearing sparkling magic shoes that would take her anywhere.

So focus on getting back to the palace to start this process that will help lift the country's economy. Rather than thinking about kisses, you should think of how you can find out as much as possible about truffle crops so you really can be of help to Rik for the short time you're here.

'Do you have books about truffle cropping in the palace?' She glanced towards the prince.

Yes, *the prince!* That was what Rik was, and Mel mustn't forget it. And since when had she started to think of him as Rik?

He said you could.

And if you have a shred of self preservation left, then you should address him as 'Your Highness' or something equally distancing, in person and in your thoughts.

'I have books at the palace and also at my personal home up in the mountains.' He glanced at her, and then up and beyond her to where those two tourists had found their way to what to Mel looked like a sheer wall of ice.

Rikardo had a second home in the mountains?

Well, duh, Mel. He's got to be about thirty and he's a prince. Did you think he'd still live permanently in a couple of rooms in the palace? Even if those rooms were quite glorious and added up to more like a small house. 'I'd like to look at the books, if that would be okay. I'd like to learn more about the industry.'

She might not be able to do anything to help with the

problems they'd had, but if Rik planned to harvest truffles from the royal grounds that, too, would be rather special. Maybe there were records about that, as well.

'The kitchen staff would have special truffle recipes, wouldn't they? Maybe handed down through the centuries? I'd love to see those!' Mel tried hard to walk normally and not lean into him. He still had hold of her arm and her silly response receptors wanted to melt into his side as though they had every right just because he'd kissed her.

He might be marrying Mel, but he was doing that to help him *avoid* a committed relationship.

And Mel was marrying him to help him out, and she didn't need to add the complication of being attracted to him to *that* mix. So it was just as well they'd shared that kiss and put it behind them. They could get on with the business end of things now.

As if it will be that easy, Mel. What about the wedding preparations? The fact that his father will think the two of you want to marry for real?

'I need to have the right things to say to your father!' The words blurted out of her with a panicky edge she didn't anticipate until it was too late to cover it up. 'That is, I don't want to be unable to answer any questions he might ask about how we met, how long we've known each other, that kind of thing.'

'We met through your cousin Nicolette when I was at university in Australia. Six months ago we came across each other on a computer forum and we've been chatting online and on the phone ever since.' He turned his head and deep blue eyes looked into hers. 'I wanted you for my princess. You are calm and pleasant and I felt I could spend the rest of my life with you. It's not the entire truth, but it's as close as we'll get.'

'Okay. That will work. I know the years that Nicolette was at university, though I didn't attend myself.' There was one other issue, though. 'What's my story? Why did I say yes?'

Before he could answer, she shook her head. 'If your father asks me that question, I'd rather tell him that I will do everything in my power to be as supportive of you as I possibly can in all the time we're together.'

He dipped his head. 'Then stick to that. Commitment to me is implied in such statements. My father should find that more than acceptable.'

'Wh-what will be expected...otherwise?' Mel asked the question tentatively, and she didn't want to be tentative. She needed to know, therefore she was asking. She straightened her spine. 'When we're married, will we be in your suite as we are now, or...?' Despite the straighter spine she couldn't quite bring herself to put it into words.

His gaze met hers. In it was steadiness. 'For the sake of appearances we would be sharing my room and... bed at first. This is something that can be managed with a little creative imagination without needing to cause you undue concern. Just for the look of things, you understand?'

'Just—just part of our overall practical arrangement. Yes. I understand totally. That's very sensible.' Mel tried not to stutter the words, tried to sound mature and au fait with the situation and what it might entail. They might be sleeping together at the start—her mind tried to boggle and she forced it not to—but they wouldn't be *sleeping together*. Not, well, you know. Not like *that*. She drew a breath. 'Right. That's okay, then. We can make that work.'

'We will, Melanie, so do not worry.' His words again held reassurance.

And Mel…relaxed into that reassurance.

They were at a turn in their downward descent where the two mountainsides faced each other when a cry ripped through the air, shattering her composure and bringing Rikardo to an abrupt stop.

'Damn. What's the man doing? He's tangled in his equipment!' Rik dumped the picnic basket and strode towards the source of the cry.

Mel followed, and after a few moments managed to spot what Rik had already seen. A man dangled against that icy outcrop. It was one of the two men she'd seen earlier. The other—Mel couldn't see.

'Stop, you fool!' Rik spoke the words aloud but they were too far away for any hope that the man might hear them.

Even so, Mel echoed the sentiment.

The prince let out a pithy curse. 'If he keeps trying to get loose, he'll drop to the bottom.' He didn't slow his pace, but he turned to glance at her. 'There's no one anywhere near except us. I've rappelled that section many times. I have to see if I can help while we wait for a rescue team to get here.'

He already had a cell phone out, and quickly called for assistance and explained the situation and that he would see what he could do until the rescue team arrived.

Mel could hear someone at the other end insisting the prince must not go anywhere near the dangerous situation, before Rik said, 'Get help here as quickly as possible' and ended the call.

She bit back the inclination to ask him if he *would* be safe enough. 'What can I do, Rik?'

'Keep yourself safe. Do not follow the path I take. Follow the path that's cut into the mountain and you'll reach the same destination. It will take longer, but I'll know you are not at risk. When the rescue team starts up the mountain, point them to where I am.' He strode ahead confidently.

Mel followed at the best pace she could manage. Each moment counted and Rik quickly got ahead of her, and then cut a different path towards the ice-bound cliff. After a few minutes she could hear him shout to the man first in English, and then in French. The conversation continued in French, and Mel could only guess what was being said.

She struggled on, determined to reach Rik and be of help if she could. She was within shouting distance herself when she looked back and saw the rescue team starting up the mountain. Mel waved to them and pointed to Rik's location, and got a wave back from the leader of the team.

Mel kept going, and then there was the man, dangling in mid-air, and Rik saying something sharp and hard to a second man at the top of the cliff before taking that man's unused equipment and kitting up.

The third prince of Braston was over the edge in a breathtakingly short time. Mel didn't go any further, then. She wasn't sure she could have if she tried. Instead she stood frozen in place, completely unable to breathe as all the concern for his safety that she'd pushed back rushed to the surface and threatened to overwhelm her.

She bit back the instinct to call out, 'Be careful.' Considering what he was doing, he would already be at the bottom of the cliff if he weren't taking care.

Nevertheless, what followed made Melanie's blood chill. She'd never watched ice rappelling. It looked risky, and it was obvious from the way he tried to control his slip that Rik didn't have the right boots on his feet for the job.

The stranded man, despite Rik's instructions that even Melanie could tell were to stay still and wait whether they were in French or not, continued to tug and pull at the tangle he was in. Did he *want* to end up at the bottom of the mountain?

'Your Highness, you must wait for us!'

'Please, Prince Rikardo, you must come away from there!'

The words were called as the rescue team came close enough to see what was happening, but it was too late. If Rik didn't do something about this man, he would kill himself. Panic had the man in its grip. The second man showed no apparent interest in proceedings, sitting there with a blank look on his face.

Had Melanie looked like that when she'd taken that medication and faded into sleep?

He's taken some kind of illicit drug, Mel. You've seen

enough of that in Melbourne to recognise it. No doubt Rik recognises it, too.

'You have to make sure that second man doesn't interfere with what Rik's doing or do anything stupid himself.' She spoke the instruction to the head of the rescue team as they drew close. 'He's under the influence of something. It's likely that both of them are, because Rik's struggling to get the stranded one to listen and stop fighting to get free.'

Rik had rappelled out beside the man. He couldn't untangle him, but he was trying to calm him. At his own risk! Even now the man reached for Rik with clawing hands!

'Oh, please, be careful,' she whispered.

She didn't notice that she'd called him Rik as she spoke to the rescue team, or that she'd spoken as though she had every right to that authority. Mel didn't care.

The next ten minutes felt like a lifetime. When the man was hauled up, Rikardo followed. He moved with confidence. Mel had made her way to the top and wanted to grab him once he got up there and…

Shake him? Check that he was unharmed?

Kiss him a second time?

'All is well, though I have asked the team to take both men to the nearest hospital and have them checked over, drug tested and, if need be, charged by the police.' Rik's words were spoken across a very calm surface.

But beneath that calm must be all the anger over the stupidity of those two men.

'Your Highness…' One of the rescue team approached.

'I am well and unharmed but you must excuse me now,' Rikardo said with respect, and firmness.

And then he stripped out of the equipment he'd commandeered, took Mel once again by the arm, and started down the mountain with her.

Mel walked at his side. 'I'm so glad you knew what to do up there. I'd like to see you do that properly one day, with all the right equipment, because I think you would be amazing at it.'

I'd like to see you do that properly one day...

Melanie's words rang in Rik's ears as he put his Italian sports car through its paces on the way to his mountain retreat home.

Her words were a salve to the anger he'd bitten back over the stupidity of those two men. Had they *wanted* to get themselves killed? The other one, when questioned, had said he was waiting for his turn to go out 'alone' and that ice rappelling was 'easy, man'.

The man had been so far gone that he hadn't even comprehended the danger his friend was in. Well, they were both safe now.

Rik let the thoughts go and turned his attention to his driving. He'd held back until he reached the private road that led to his home. This road, he knew better than the back of his hand, every turn, just how much he could give behind the wheel to release the pent-up energy that came from that stressful rappel in someone else's untested equipment. He'd needed this.

He's going too fast. Mel couldn't get the thought out of her head. Her logical mind understood that Rik had control of the car. It was clear he knew this road well. The road itself was wide with plenty of room for dual traffic and yet it was a private road. They hadn't seen any other cars and she guessed they were quite un-likely to do so.

All of this made infinite sense. The paralysing fear inside Mel did not make sense. Her fingers curled into the edges of her seat. Her heart pounded with a mixture of apprehension and the need to get out of this situa-tion at any cost.

'Please stop.' The words whispered through her clenched teeth, whispered so quietly that she didn't know how Rik could have heard them.

All Mel knew was that she wanted out of this car. Now.

'Melanie.' A voice tinged with remorse broke through her fear. The car began immediately to slow and Rik said, 'I'm sorry. I didn't realise you were uncomfort-able.'

It's all right. I'm fine. There's no need to slow down or stop.

In her mind, Mel entertained these polite thoughts. But her instincts were in a very different place. She struggled to breathe normally, to not throw her door open and try to get out. The reaction was so intense and so deep that it completely unnerved her. She couldn't speak, couldn't think clearly, didn't know what to say to him, didn't understand why she had ended up feel-ing like this.

Within moments the car moved much more slowly and fingers wrapped firmly around the hand nearest to him. 'Do you need me to stop the car completely, Melanie? My house is less than a minute away and I'd rather get you there if possible.'

The roaring in her ears started to recede but Mel was still a long way from calm. Her fingers tightened around his. 'I don't know what came over me. I feel stupid for the way I've reacted.'

'You are certainly not stupid.' Rik spoke these words softly as he drew the car to a stop in front of his mountain home. The place was maintained for him, but did not have permanent staff. They would be alone here, and he was glad for that now to give Melanie a chance to recover.

Whatever had happened during the trip had affected her deeply, and he felt she would benefit from space and not having to deal with anyone new just for the moment.

Had the panic come on because of all the pressure he'd put on her? It was a lot to ask a woman to become his temporary princess, to work with him to fool his father into believing the marriage was intended to last a lifetime.

It was a lot for her to find herself here under confused circumstances let alone the pressure Rik had added to that load for her.

You must take care of her. Give her time to calm down.

He got out of the car, opened her door for her and took her hand to help her out. His home was chalet-style, built of log and with a sharply pitched roof. Large windows gave beautiful views from every part of the home and were one-way tinted for privacy. Rik doubted that Melanie noticed any of it. Her face was sheet-white and the hand he held within his trembled.

'Let me get you a hot drink, Melanie.' He led her inside and to a comfortable leather sofa in the living room.

'Thank you. It is a bit chilly, isn't it?' Melanie sank onto the sofa and didn't argue about who should be preparing the beverages.

Rik didn't waste time, and quickly returned with coffee for both of them. He took his seat beside her. 'This will take the chill away.'

The rooms were centrally heated, but she'd clearly had a shock. It would take time for her body to return to a normal temperature.

Rik had brought that shock about. He had put too much on her. Bringing her to Braston with her waking up from a long sleep to discover she was in the middle of Europe instead of in Sydney. He'd asked her to replace her cousin and briefly marry him. Had piled all the worries about the country onto her, and then had left her to cope with her concern for him while he rappelled onto an icy cliff in dangerous circumstances to deal with a man who didn't want to hear reason, and another who could have added more trouble to the mix.

To cap it off, Rik had come up here to get away from things, and the speed of his driving had frightened her enough that she hadn't been able to even tell him what was wrong.

As Melanie sipped her coffee and colour began to come back into her face Rik set his drink down and turned to her. 'I am sorry that you were afraid during the drive up here.'

'You weren't to know that I would react like that. I didn't know it myself.' She forced her gaze about the room before meeting his eyes. For the first time since leaving the car, she seemed to see her surroundings.

Maybe that, too, helped her, because she said valiantly, 'It was worth the trip. This is a lovely home and the views are amazing. And I feel much better. I'm sure I won't have that kind of problem again.'

'I am pleased that you're starting to feel better. What happened to you? Do car trips always make you uneasy?'

Back in Australia, she'd checked when he collected her from outside Nicolette's home that he felt fresh enough to drive. Rik hadn't thought anything of it.

'That's the first time I've been in a sports car. They go very fast.' As she seemed to consider what had happened she frowned. 'I don't understand this myself. I don't drive, but I'm not usually the type to panic unnecessarily, and with hindsight I *know* that you had control of what you were doing.

'I'm just sorry that I spoiled the drive for you,' she said. 'You obviously needed an outlet after dealing with those two foolish men and keeping your calm so well, both before and after.'

Rik *had* needed that outlet. Sometimes keeping his cool came at a cost to his blood pressure!

'I felt like telling them off myself for being so stupid,' she added hotly, 'and I wasn't the one who had to risk life and limb to go out and stop that first man from falling to his death!'

Maybe if she learned to drive herself, she might feel better informed and more confident to assess the skill of other drivers when they were behind the wheel.

They were side by side on the sofa, and Rik became very conscious of that as they fell silent and gave their attention to their drinks.

After a moment, she spoke with a slight teasing tone in her voice. 'You make very good coffee. Is it allowed, for a prince of the realm to do such tasks as make coffee?'

'And do them well?' He shrugged his shoulders. 'I think in today's world it is, and I would go hungry and thirsty up here if it weren't.'

She was a plucky girl. Resilient. The thoughts came to Rik and lodged. He couldn't help but admire her for that.

'Do you think I could have a tour while we're here?' she asked. 'I'd love to see the rest of your home.'

'Absolutely.' Rik got to his feet and held out his hand to help Melanie rise.

He was getting in the habit of that, of reaching for her hand far too often...

But you will need to do things like that to make the upcoming marriage plans seem realistic to your father.

Even though Georgio would not expect it to be a love match, he would still expect such demonstrations.

'The meeting with my father has not yet been arranged. I think it can wait for a little longer yet.' Rik drew a breath. 'I'd like some time to restore a better mood before I tackle that talk, to be honest.'

'Then I'm glad I asked for the tour.' Mel melted the moment Rik confessed his need to prepare for the talk with his father. And she truly did feel so much better now. 'We can stay here as long as you want. It's a beautiful place.'

Rik was good company and they'd just sort of got engaged, so why shouldn't they stay here for a bit, if they wanted to? She could use the time to ask a few questions about how they would work their way through the next few months, too.

'I'll need a wedding dress.' Visions of past royal marriages scrolled through her mind. 'Something very simple that won't cost the earth.' She turned to Rik. 'How do we pull off a wedding in a month?'

'With a really good wedding planner, and, as you've already realised, with the most simplified plans possible.' He started towards the rear of the house and said firmly, 'Now let me show you the rest of my retreat, and all the views. I think they're worth seeing.'

They were, and Mel looked out of floor-length windows at some very lovely scenery before Rik toured her through the rest of his home. It was surprisingly humble. Well, not humble. It was a delightful four-bedroom chalet-style home but it certainly wasn't, well, a palace.

'I love this place,' she blurted. 'If it was me I'd be up here all the time. Normal-sized rooms, calm atmosphere, no one to tell you what to do.'

'You've just worked out the secrets of my attraction to this home.' He smiled and led her into the final room.

It was an office, with a desk and computer and shelves of books about... 'Oh. Can I look at some of those? Do you have ones that show what the truffles look like when they're harvested? History books? Anything about the *royal* truffles? Cooking? The growth process from beginning to end and the uses of truffle hogs?'

'Yes to all of that. And I trained Rufusina under the tutelage of Winnow. There is a photo album.' Rik brought out the photo album and a selection of books and before Mel knew it she was nose down in some gorgeous pictures, and some very interesting information. He didn't have cookbooks, but he told her that some of the old recipes were still produced at the palace and described some of the dishes.

'Truffled turkey. I'd like to cook that.' Mel thought back through her cooking career. 'The closest I've come to cooking with truffles is using truffle-flavoured oil a few times.'

Rik's brows lifted. 'You had a career as a cook?'

'Yes, working for my aunt and uncle.' Mel glanced at him through her lashes. She'd thought he would have known that already.

They were seated with her on the swivel chair, and him leaning back against the corner of the desk in his office. It wasn't a large room, and as she let herself register the cosiness, his closeness, Mel suddenly became breathless. 'I cooked for them for years. Cakes and desserts were my speciality, but I cooked all the meals, including for dinner parties. They liked to schmooze wealthy—'

She coughed and turned her attention back to the books. 'These are wonderful resources. It's an intricate industry. You've done well to get the black truffles growing commercially here.'

'Not so well in the past two years.' Rik glanced up and towards the windows.

The frown that came to his face made Mel follow his glance.

She hadn't noticed the change in atmosphere, but now she saw it. 'I didn't know it had started snowing.'

'Yes.' He got up from the desk. 'Why don't you select what books you'd like to bring back to the palace when we return, while I see what's in the kitchen that we can have for our lunch?'

Not that Mel minded either way and it wasn't as though Rik were trying to trap her into spending time with him here. He'd probably enjoy the time away from the palace while he could, but would have been just as content to be up here by himself.

Something in his expression still made her ask. 'How long do you think it will snow?'

CHAPTER SIX

IT SNOWED all that day. When darkness fell, Rik closed the curtains throughout his chalet home and turned to face Mel.

While Rik appeared completely calm Mel couldn't say the same. She stood rather uncertainly in the middle of the living room.

With the prince. Up here in his chalet where he'd just made the decision that they wouldn't be leaving until morning. So they would be here. All alone. Together. For all that time.

'It won't matter too much?' She asked the question in a deliberately businesslike tone that somehow managed to emerge sounding chatty and confiding and breathless all at once. Mel forged on. 'That you can't get back tonight, I mean?'

Even despite the tone, Mel would have said she did well, that the question was at least focused on whether he might have problems because he couldn't attend to duties at the palace tonight.

Yes. That was a good way to put it. 'Your duties—?' Really, she felt quite relaxed about this whole situation.

After all they were just staying in a different location for a night. She'd slept in a bedroom within Rik's suite of rooms last night, which was rather intimate when you thought about it, and that hadn't bothered her.

Not even when you leapt out of bed the next morning because you could hear him speaking just outside your closed door? Because you wanted to get through the shower and look your best for him before he saw you? Because you hadn't been entirely certain whether he'd pulled the covers over you the night before when you might not have looked your best?

'It won't matter at all. I gave Dominico another quick call while I was outside checking the snowfall. He'll take care of anything urgent until I get back tomorrow morning.' His cheek creased as he gave a lopsided and quite devastating smile. *He* didn't seem at all concerned or put out by their circumstances.

Which was great, of course.

That was exactly how Mel would feel in a moment when she finished pushing away these silly thoughts about being up here alone with him and how that might impact on the rest of the evening. It must be because he had kissed her on the mountainside earlier. Or because they'd spent the afternoon poring over truffle books and photo albums that showed many shots of Rufusina being trained by Rik and Rik laughing in some of the shots.

Perhaps it was also because she would be pretending to be engaged and then married to him.

'We'll end up holding hands and kissing…' Somehow the words were attached to the blood vessels in her face.

Heat swept upwards from her neck and rushed into her cheeks.

'Yes,' Rik said in a deep voice. 'At times we...will.'

Rikardo. Prince Rikardo. You'll end up holding hands and kissing Prince Rikardo.

Oh, as though putting it in the correct words made it any better!

Even the reminder didn't hold the weight it should have, and Mel just didn't know what to do about that. Something had happened when he took her hand and got her out of the car and brought her inside and made her a hot drink and set to work to help her get past the ridiculous fear she'd experienced.

He acted just like your dream idea of a very ordinary man, showing a sensitive side while still being very, very strong and being wonderful and appealing and all the things you might want—

But Mel didn't want a man. Well, not for a long time. Not like that in the way of settling down together and falling in love so she ended up vulnerable. She wasn't ready for that! The thought burst through, and was somehow linked to her earlier panic while trapped in the speeding car with Rik.

Maybe she just felt panicky at the moment, full stop.

Maybe she needed to focus on right now because this was enough of a challenge, thanks very much!

Rikardo wasn't an ordinary man anyway. Mel couldn't afford to forget that.

Not while reading truffle books and smiling over Rufusina photos. Not while kissing him on a mountainside because that had been a kiss to seal a bargain.

It might have blown her away, but he'd just kissed her and that had been that. Probably checking to make sure he could make it look believable any time they had to repeat the exercise over the next month and the months after that.

How many times might they…?

Mel's heart tripped.

She contemplated turning into a contortionist so she could kick herself for being so silly. The next months would be businesslike as often as possible. That was what they would be. Now what had they been saying? 'Evening in. Yes. That'll be fine. The only thing that matters is that it doesn't interfere with other plans of yours. The treatment in the truffle groves—has that been done today or do you need to be there to supervise it? That's the one thing I didn't ask about while we studied those books.'

'Winnow has supervised the treatment today. He knows what to do, and Dominico organised payment to cover it.' He brushed this aside as though it were irrelevant.

Not the treatment part, the money part. Was it? Mel hadn't got the impression that the money would come out of some endless royal coffer. If that could happen then Rik wouldn't be stressing over getting the people out of financial trouble to the degree that he was. He'd said that there needed to be reform.

Her eyes narrowed. Had he paid for that treatment himself somehow? Out of money that perhaps shouldn't be invested in that direction because it was for his personal use or he'd earned it himself? She knew so little about him and she wanted to know…everything?

Purely because Mel preferred to understand the people she dealt with!

'We'll treat tonight as an evening off,' he declared. 'If the remainder of this month is very busy, we can remember that we at least had a few hours to—how do you say it? "Veg out and do nothing."'

'Why, yes.' A delighted laugh escaped Mel. She couldn't help it. The sound just flew out. Mel also couldn't drag her gaze from that crease in his cheek, or from the sparkle in his deep blue eyes.

So she gave in and let herself enjoy the moment. It wasn't as though Rik would want to spend the entire night kissing her senseless just because they were alone.

Just because he'd kissed her once already. Just because he was the best kisser she'd ever been kissed by and there would be times in the public eye, at least, when he would kiss her again. Just because he made her want to don sparkly shoes *and* leap into a rabbit hole.

'If we're having a night in,' a night of not kissing each other, 'then I guess we just need to work out how we want to spend our time.'

'Not reading about truffles.' This too was said with a smile.

Oh, she could fall heavily for that smile. She wouldn't, though. Not when she'd reminded herself that she was doing this to help him, and help the people of Braston, and because she'd ended up here by mistake and there weren't a lot of other options for him now, like none at all really, and she could afford the time and effort to help. Did it really make any difference whether she started her new life in Sydney this week or four months from now?

'I think I've taken in as much information about truffles as I can manage for one day, but I'm pleased to know more about the industry. It's obviously really important—to—to people here.' She'd almost said that it was important to Rik, and that was why she'd wanted to understand.

That wouldn't be the key reason, of course. She wanted to be supportive of Rik's efforts. She'd made the commitment to marry him for that reason. But she wasn't obsessing over learning all about his life and work or anything like that.

Are you sure about that, Melanie? Because you seem mightily interested in him, really.

Yes, she was sure! And no she was not ridiculously interested! She was helping to fix a problem that she was partially responsible for creating in the first place. She was no more interested than she should be.

'It's a fascinating industry,' she said in the most dampening tone she could muster. 'The truffle industry. But perhaps we could pass the time this evening some other way?'

Like snuggling on the sofa?

No. Like…well, she didn't know. Cooking? Playing on the Internet?

'How do you feel about television?' Rik indicated the large screen in the corner of the room. 'I have a selection of DVDs I've not yet got around to watching.'

'Watching DVDs would be…' *Smart. Sensible. Safe?*

Better than thinking about kissing the whole night? 'A good idea. I don't mind a good comedy, but I'll watch most things.'

They sat on the floor in front of the DVD cabinet going through choices until she found episodes of an Australian comedy show she hadn't yet watched. 'Oh, you have this series! I've only ever seen a few episodes but it's supposed to be brilliant!'

So they sat side by side on the sofa with popcorn that Rik made in the microwave, and sodas from his fridge, and watched comedy episodes until Mel had giggled so many times that she'd forgotten to feel self-conscious at all in Rik's presence. Instead she had become totally enamoured of the rich, deep rumble that accounted for *his* laughter.

And she forgot to guard against letting herself be aware of him as an attractive appealing man and not a prince who should be held at arm's length because she was only here for a few months and he was marrying her so he could avoid any kind of commitment to a woman, even if Mel didn't know why he seemed to need to do that as much as he needed to. They were almost through the evening, anyway.

So why are you almost holding your breath, Mel, as though waiting for something to happen?

'Goodnight, Mel.' Rik walked Melanie to the opened doorway of her bedroom.

They'd watched their comedy episodes. Mel had paid more attention than he had. Did she feel it the way that he did? This compulsion that ate at him to draw closer, know her, use every avenue and every moment to learn more of her and to let her learn more of him? And a coinciding physical consciousness that seemed to fill the air around them with a charge of electricity just waiting for one small spark to set it ablaze?

Why did this woman make him feel this way more than any other had? Rik didn't want to admit that to himself, but he forced the acknowledgement.

Then admit that you desire her, and that the desire is as much about her personality as it is about her physical appeal.

He'd spent this evening with her and he'd thought about how different their lives were and mad thoughts had come through his mind about bridging the gaps.

Look how well longevity and sticking together had worked for his father and mother. The queen had walked out, had done the one thing Rik and his brothers had never expected. She had turned her back on what she had treated as the core of her duty. And now neither parent would discuss the matter with their sons.

Rik turned his thoughts back to the present.

At times today Mel seemed to have almost forgotten that Rik was a prince. He'd…liked that. But now was not a good time for him to forget the arrangement they'd made. He needed this to work. To be distracted by her beauty and appeal was not the right thing for him to do, to be distracted mentally and in *liking* her so much, even less smart because it spoke of an emotional awareness that couldn't happen. Rik could never trust…

'Good—goodnight, Rik.' She said the words quietly, almost tentatively.

With a question in their depths?

Her small hand came to rest on his forearm and she reached up and briefly kissed his cheek. 'I'll see you in the morning and I'll be ready for whatever needs to be done to help get your temporary marriage plans started, or just to keep out of the way if you need to work in the truffle groves tomorrow.'

Rik searched her face and saw the determination to do the right thing, to dismiss him and her awareness of him at one and the same time. To remain Melanie here and Rikardo there and never the two should cross over their lines.

He saw all that, and he *felt* what was inside her. A very different compulsion that he felt, too, that made him want to lean in and replace that pseudo-kiss with the real thing. To know for himself if the last kiss had been some kind of strange fluke. If her lips would taste as good a second time.

'Sleep well.' He turned and started for his room at the end of the short corridor. 'I will see you in the morning. Thank you for your company this evening. I… really enjoyed it.'

And with that, Prince Rikardo Eduard Ettonbierre of Braston went to his room, stepped inside and shut the door firmly behind him.

Only then did he lift his hand to allow his fingertips to lightly trace where her lips had pressed to his cheek.

It was perfectly fine for him to find Melanie likeable, and to still marry her, end the marriage short months later, and get on with the single life that he wanted, and *needed* to maintain.

He *would not* be marrying for real.

Rik sighed and dropped his hand. For now he needed to prepare for bed.

Tomorrow was a new day and no doubt a new set of challenges.

CHAPTER SEVEN

'I WOULD like to present to you my fiancée, Nicole Melanie Watson.' Rik spoke the words to King Georgio formally, and as though the other impromptu meeting had never occurred. 'My fiancée is known by her middle name of Melanie.'

If the occasion had been less formal, Mel might have smiled at Rik's tweaking of history to suit himself. But this was not that kind of moment. Mel curtsied.

'I am pleased to meet you, Melanie.' Georgio took her hand and air-kissed above the fingers and, while doing so, searched her face. After a moment he gave a slight nod and indicated a setting of leather lounges and chairs to the left.

They were in what Rik referred to as one of the 'great rooms'. It was a large area, and could have felt intimidating if Mel hadn't walked in here determined *not* to be intimidated.

Mel and Rik had made their way down the mountain this morning. He'd driven at a gentler pace and Mel had remained calm until they were almost at the palace. Nervous anticipation had set in then but Mel felt that was justified.

'Let us get to know one another a little, Melanie,' Georgio said as they all took their seats.

Rik sat on one of the sofas beside Mel. He seemed deeply resolved this morning. Last night, when she'd thought he would kiss her at her door, kiss her *properly*, Melanie had thought he might feel as confused and tempted and aware of her as she did of him. But of course that was quite silly. He might have wanted to kiss her. But that didn't mean his emotions were engaged.

Not that Mel's were!

Concentrate on the king, Mel. This is not the time for anything else.

'Melanie and I first met through a cousin of hers.' Rik added a few details.

When the king nodded, Mel bit back the urge to heave a sigh of relief. But she also had to handle her share of the conversation. 'I admire Rikardo, and the work that he does for the people of Braston. I want to be as supportive of that as I possibly can.'

'That is good.' Georgio's glance shifted from Mel to Rik and back to Mel again. 'And what did you do before you agreed to marry my son?'

'I worked as a cook.' It might not have been a glamorous job. It would probably sound even less glamorous if she admitted she had done that for little money, working for her relatives to earn her right to a sense of belonging.

Note to self, Mel. You never did earn that right and you waited too long to get yourself out of that situation.

A similar set of rites was being played out in this room between Rik and his father.

She turned the highest wattage smile she could muster towards King Georgio. 'My history is humble, I suppose, but there's nothing to be ashamed of in coming from everyday stock.'

'If that "stock" has an appropriate history attached to it.' Georgio's eyes narrowed. 'My son will run a check. I will see this report for myself.'

Like a police-record check or something?

No, Mel, it will be a lot more detailed even than that.

She tried not to bristle at the thought, and at the king's emotionless declaration. As though he did this all the time and would have no hesitation in eliminating her like a blot from Rik's radar screen if she didn't come up to standard.

It didn't actually matter whether Georgio liked her or approved of her or not, provided she could marry Rik so that Rik could carry out his plans.

I still don't like it. My family history is my business. I don't want it exposed to all and sundry.

'Dominico already ran the check.' Rik clipped the words off. 'You may take Melanie at her word, Father. There is nothing in her history to justify the need for you to view the report.'

Mel stiffened inwardly for a second time.

Rik leaned close to her and said softly, 'I'm sorry. It was necessary. Dominico gave me a very light summary of the report.'

Much of Mel's agitation subsided. 'I don't have anything to hide. I just don't like the idea...'

'Of your privacy being invaded.' The twist to his lips was ironic.

Somehow that irony helped Mel to let the matter go.

Georgio straightened slightly in his chair. 'I could order a search of my own.'

A chill formed in the edges of Rik's deep blue irises. 'But I think you will agree there is no need.'

For a moment as father and son locked gazes the room filled with the powerful clash of two strong wills. It occurred to Mel then that there were matters within such families that were very different from 'regular' life. Yes, Rik had ordered a search of her life and history. No, she hadn't liked hearing that. But if Rik hadn't done the search, his father would have ordered it. At least this way Mel wasn't exposed to Georgio reading the entire report.

A moment later Georgio glanced away. Rik had won that round, it was done and the conversation moved on to more general topics.

Rik raised the matter of the truffle harvest. Mel sat quietly listening, but she remained aware of Georgio's examination.

No way would he have accepted a switch between her and her cousin. He was too observant.

So you've done the right thing, Mel, by agreeing to help Rik. And Georgio is a strong-willed man and very set in his attitudes. You're helping Rik to avoid being pushed into a long-term loveless marriage for the wrong reasons, too.

* * *

'You have done well this morning, Melanie. I'm proud of you.' Rik spoke the words and then realised it perhaps wasn't his place to feel such an emotion in the rather personal way that he did towards his fiancée right now. She wasn't marrying him for real reasons. She was doing this to help him and she understood that it would all end a few months from now.

Tell her what the buy-off will be in exchange for her assistance.

The thought came, and Rik…pushed it aside once again, for later. He would take care of Melanie, would ensure that she got good assistance to start her on her way with her new life in Sydney when she returned to Australia. When the moment was right to bring the topic up, he would do so. He…felt that she would know inherently that he would…take care of her.

Rik used a key to unlock the door to a small room. 'There will be a number of rings you can choose from for your engagement ring.'

'From the family h-heirlooms?' Mel's footsteps faltered in the doorway.

For a moment Rik thought she might back out of the room, refuse to enter. 'They are not all heirlooms,' he said, 'but yes.'

She drew a deep breath, threw her shoulders back and continued into the room. 'It's probably a good idea to use something from the family's stock of jewellery. The ring can be given back when we're finished, and it won't have cost you anything. We need to find one that fits and doesn't need adjusting, and that you wouldn't choose if you were—'

Doing this for real.

The words echoed unspoken in the room.

The practicality of her determined attitude made Rik want to smile, and yet when they stepped fully into the room and he saw the spread of jewellery that Dominico had laid out for them, a strange feeling swept over him. His gaze shifted from piece to piece until he found a ring that he felt would suit Mel. A ring that he would have chosen for her if their circumstances had been different?

There *were* no different circumstances possible, either now or in his future. Yet to Rik in this moment—

He lifted a ring with a platinum band. The three diamonds were Asscher cut to reflect light off the many facets. The stones were perfectly round, and set with the larger of the three diamonds raised higher than the two to its left and right. Because the ring was simple and the setting not as high as some, the size of the diamonds did not leap out as it might have.

The platinum band would suit Melanie's colouring; the setting would look beautiful on her finger. It was a ring he could enjoy seeing on her for decades.

Well, it would do for the time being. He lifted the ring. 'This was not an engagement ring, but a dress ring of my grandmother that she had fashioned for her later in her life. Her fingers were small and delicate as yours are. I do not know if she ever even wore it. She was rather indulgent when it came to such creations. I...feel the ring may suit you.'

'Oh.' Melanie didn't even glance at the remaining

jewellery. And when Rik took her hand gently in his and slipped the ring onto her finger, she caught her breath. Her gaze flew to his. 'It—it fits perfectly. Just as though—'

'Just as though,' he murmured, and there, in the quiet of a small room filled with valuable jewellery that Melanie had been hesitant to go anywhere near, Rik lifted her hand and kissed the finger upon which his engagement ring now rested.

'Just as though we were a real engaged couple, I was going to say.' She whispered the words and glanced down at the ring. 'I didn't expect it to look—'

Right. She hadn't expected it to look right. Rik didn't need her to finish the sentence to know that was what she'd meant to say. He hadn't expected it either. Nor had he expected the sudden sense of well-being and destiny that swept over him when he placed the ring on her finger.

Was he getting in over his head with her somehow despite his determination to treat this as a business transaction? Had he allowed some attitudes and thoughts to slide in wrong directions because, if he hadn't, then how had he ended up with such unexpected feelings in the first place?

Rik should have been sorting out the answers to those questions. Instead he leaned towards her and somehow his arm was around her, drawing her close.

This time when he kissed her it was he who lost himself in a moment that should not have been, lost himself in the taste and texture and the giving of

Melanie's lips as he kissed her until he had to break away or—

It would all feel far too real?

You cannot let it become that way, Rikardo. Melanie is a sweet girl, but she never will be more than a means to an end. You will never marry permanently, not for real and not for love, and not to lock yourself for ever into a loveless marriage.

He would never trust such an emotion as 'love' within that institution. Not when his parents hadn't managed even to love their sons let alone each other.

'I have something else that I wish to show you this morning.' Rik escorted her from the room, Away from a room full of the beauty that should go with emotion and dreams and the love of a lifetime, but had it ever existed within his family? There was that old legend, but…

Rik increased his pace.

'Th-thank you for the beautiful choice of ring, Rik,' Mel said softly as they stepped out of doors and started along an outside pathway that led between vast stretches of snow-covered grounds.

On her finger, the ring felt light and comfortable. It fitted perfectly and maybe that was what disturbed Mel so much. That and the fact that *Rik* had chosen it out of a dazzling array of royal jewellery. Rik had wanted her to wear *this* ring, and then he'd kissed her. It was the second time they'd sealed their agreement with a kiss, and each time became more difficult to treat as just a meeting of lips against lips.

What kind of state would she be in by the time he kissed her on the wedding day?

'I should not have kissed you like that.' His glance meshed momentarily with hers.

Had he read her mind? Considering the messy confused state of the thoughts in there, she hoped not!

Rik went on. 'Our arrangement is not for…that kind of purpose and I should have remembered.'

'Well, it was probably because we'd just been with your father and working so hard to make sure that all went well.' She gave a laugh that sounded just a bit forced. 'We got a little too carried away in our roles but it was only for a moment. It probably barely left an impression, really.'

Her words were just making this worse! She bit her lip. Mel glanced about them and her gaze fell on a small piece of machinery ahead. 'That's an interesting-looking vehicle.'

Rik followed Melanie's gaze.

She was wise to change the topic. He was more than happy to work with her in that respect, though his glance did drop again to her hand where the ring sat as though it belonged there, and then to her soft lips, which had yielded so beautifully beneath his just moments ago. He wanted to kiss her again. Kiss and so much more.

Not happening, Rik.

And yet his instincts told him that the kisses they'd shared had been far more than instantly forgettable to her.

To him, too, if he were honest.

'This is an all-weather buggy.' He explained that

Winnow had taken the vehicle out of storage and made sure it was in working order. 'In first gear it doesn't drive any faster than a person can walk. It's easy to handle. All you need to do is steer and make it stop and start. It will drive on snow and it can handle rough terrain but there are plenty of paths here to drive it on. Our appointment with the wedding planner is not for another hour. I thought I might show you how to work this while we wait.'

Her gaze flew to his. 'You want me to drive it?'

'I thought it might be a good way for you to start to be able to get around more while you're here.' In truth there were a dozen ways he could ensure that Melanie could move around the area, and for the most part Rik expected to be with her anyway. Even so...

'I don't drive cars.' She said it quickly, and then tipped her head to the side and looked at the buggy, and back at Rik. 'I've never really had any interest in learning.'

'This is not a car.' He watched her face, and took a gamble. 'But if you don't feel that you can try it—'

Her chin went up. 'Of course I'll try it. That would be like saying I didn't want to try riding a skateboard or making some new dish in the kitchen.'

She was a plucky girl, his Melanie, Rik thought. Before he could pull himself up on the possessive manner of wording that thought, Melanie stepped forward and did an at least passable job of feigning delight at the idea of learning all about the buggy.

'First I will demonstrate.' Rik sat in the driving seat

with Melanie beside him and showed her the controls. They were on castle grounds in an area where the worst that could happen was they ended up off the path. He got the buggy moving, explaining as he drove, and then, when he felt Mel was ready, Rik simply got out of the seat and started walking beside her. 'Slide into the driver's seat.'

Mel slid over and gripped the wheel. A moment later she was steering the buggy grimly.

He guided her along, helping her to master steering around corners and stopping and starting. After a few minutes Mel didn't need his help, and even asked if he would get back in with her so she could increase speed to a higher gear.

Finally her hands unclenched and she gave the first hint of a smile before she stopped the buggy and turned to look at him.

'Well done,' he praised. 'I am glad you have been able to do this, Mel.'

'It was fun. It's such a long time since I've completely enjoyed anything that resembled vehicle travel. All the way back to when my parents used to take me every Sunday and we'd go...' Her expression sobered and she frowned as though trying to remember something.

Though she tried to conceal it, sadness touched her face. She climbed out of the buggy. 'I don't remember what we used to do. They...died in a car crash.'

His hand wrapped around her fingers, enclosing her. He wished he could warm her heart from that chill. He wanted to do that for her so much. 'I am sorry—'

'It's all right. It was a long time ago.' Her words relegated her pain to the past. But her fingers wrapped around his…

A member of the palace staff approached to let Rik know that the wedding planner had arrived. The moment ended, but the tenderness Rik felt for Melanie grew inside him.

Duty. He had to attend to his duty.

Rik dipped his head. 'Please tell the planner we will be with her shortly.'

'Yes, Prince Rikardo.' The man walked away.

Melanie turned her gaze towards Rik and drew a deep breath. 'This is the next phase, isn't it? We have to convince this planner that we're doing this for real, even if we do want a simple, quick, trouble-free arrangement.' She seemed to think about what she'd just said, and a thoughtful expression came over her face. 'You must have chosen a great planner, if the woman believes she can achieve that, in a month, for a royal wedding of any description.'

Rik drew a slow breath as his gaze examined her face, flushed with the success of learning to drive the buggy, and her expressive eyes that had clouded when the topic of her parents had come up.

Perhaps he should ask Dominico for a proper look at that report after all. It might tell Rik more about Melanie's background.

Only to help understand her, he justified, and then frowned because, of all reasons he might read the report, wasn't that the most personal and therefore to him, at least, the most unacceptable? 'Dominico seems to believe this planner will be up to the task. Let us go see how she fares with our requests.'

CHAPTER EIGHT

'You have made very rapid plans, Rik.'

'Are you sure you want to marry so quickly? Our father might still have given us what we wanted if we all became engaged and then spoke to him again about the arrangement. That way you could have held off from actually marrying until closer to the six-months mark. Things might have changed by then.'

The words came to Melanie in two different male voices as she went in search of Rik. It was four days later and she'd woken to find her breakfast waiting for her, and Rik already gone to the palace grounds to oversee the harvesting of the first of the special truffles.

'It won't make any difference whether I marry soon, or marry after many months. You know this. Our father will not change his mind or soften his expectations.'

Rik didn't explain the reason for his statement—the brief nature of the intended marriage—and Mel didn't know if he'd told his brothers the truth about it as yet or not. But did his voice sound oddly flat *because* he knew this fact?

She must be imagining it.

You and your over-inflated ego are imagining it to-gether, Mel.

'Good—good morning, Rikardo.' Mel spoke to make her presence known. Not because she minded her impending marriage to Rik being discussed, but because it wasn't right to eavesdrop, even if she hadn't meant to.

'Melanie. I am glad you're awake and have found us.' Rik stepped forward. He touched her hand and gestured to the two men standing to their left. 'These are my brothers, Marcelo and Anrai.'

'Hello. I'm pleased to meet you both.' The words emerged in a calm tone before Mel stopped to remember that she was being introduced to two more princes.

Rabbit hole. Sparkly shoes. Do I look good enough for this occasion, and why didn't I address him as Prince Rikardo or Your Highness?

She drew a breath.

'It is a delight to meet you, Melanie. Our brother has told us about you.' The older man bowed over her hand and managed to make the gesture seem relaxed and European rather than princely and…royal. 'I am Marcelo.'

The first in line to the throne. The brother who would most of all be expected to marry and stay married, whether he wanted to or not. He was dark like Rik, a little taller, and his eyes were such a deep inky blue, they were almost black.

'I am Anrai.' The second brother smiled a killer smile, shook her hand, and stepped back as though content to observe proceedings from this point. His hair was a lighter brown, thick and with a slight wave.

It flopped over his forehead and drew attention to sparkling pale blue eyes.

Mel had dismissed him as not as handsome as Rik. She could now see that he would actually be a quite stunning lady-killer, but he still didn't appeal to *her*. She only had eyes for—

'Hello.' Mel tried to smile naturally and not feel overwhelmed by being surrounded by these three very royal men. It wasn't until she glanced at Rik's face that she realised she'd placed herself so close to his side that they were almost touching. Not because she felt intimidated but because…

Well, she couldn't explain it, actually. What she did realise was that she'd been allowing herself to think of Rik more as a man, and less as a prince. At least this meeting had given her that reality check. And it was nice to meet his brothers. 'Have any of the truffles been dug out yet?'

A snort from behind them drew Mel's attention. She turned her head and there was Rufusina. The pig had a quilted coat on and a keen look in her eyes, as though she was sitting in apparent obedience waiting for something.

'Rufusina's obviously champing at the snout,' Mel observed. 'What's the hold-up?'

'There's no hold-up—' Rik started.

'We were just deciding how best to go about the extraction,' Anrai added.

Marcelo's brows formed a vee. 'It is the most stupid thing to wait for a sign from—'

Rufusina lifted her snout, sniffed the air once, and then again.

Rik said under his breath, 'Wait for it.'

Anrai's shoulders stiffened.

The truffle hog sniffed the air a third time and trotted to a group of trees.

'*Now* I will go in there.' Anrai followed Rufusina's rapidly receding form. 'But only because I think she knows where the best truffles are. It has nothing to do with anything else.'

'Marcelo?' Rik turned to his older brother.

'I was not concerned in the first instance.' The oldest brother followed Anrai. 'All the truffles on the palace grounds are exceptional, as has been proved in years past. That is all that matters.'

Rik turned to Mel. 'Would you care to be present while Rufusina does her work and finds us the choicest truffles?'

'I would love to be there.' Mel's curiosity was tweaked. Just what had that "rite of passage" been about? And to be present while such wonderful foods were lifted from their resting places? Imagine *tasting* such a wonderful, rare indulgence!

Rik took her arm and started towards a grove of trees that looked very old. 'It is an exciting moment.'

'Apologies, Melanie, for walking away.' Anrai rubbed the back of his neck with his hand. 'Once the pig sniffs the air three times—'

'It will guide the prince to truffles that are the choicest, and that are possessed of the power to make his deepest hopes come true.' Marcelo said the words with a dismissive twist of his lips. 'You must forgive us, Melanie. We are being foolish this morning, but Rikardo—'

'Asked nicely if you would both like to be present for this event.' Rik jumped in with the words that were almost defensive.

Mel thought about her rabbit hole and the sparkly shoes and how out of place she'd felt when she arrived here, and how different this world was from anything she had ever known. And she looked at three big, brave men who had hovered at the edge of a grove of trees and refused to shift until...

'A magic truffle hog unlocks the key to safe passage, and perhaps to the granting of your wishes?' The words came with the start of a smile that spread until it almost cracked her face in half.

She could have laughed aloud. Mel could have done a lot of things. But then she looked properly at the grove of trees and thought about age and history. Three princes *had* all come to participate in this ritual. Rufusina *had* lifted her nose and sniffed three times and then trotted over here with purpose. Mel sobered. 'How old is the legend? Are there bad aspects attached if you don't do things the right way?'

'Centuries. None of us have ever come near the harvesting of these truffles until now. It's usually left to our staff, but I wanted to oversee it this time.' Rik didn't seem offended by her initial amusement. He did seem a little uncomfortable having to explain the situation. 'The legend is more to do with prosperous lives, and making the right choice of marriages and so on. But I am only concerned with getting good truffles for my overseas buyers.'

'Yes. That is no doubt the priority.' Mel bit back any further smiles. She turned to the others and said to all three of them, 'I'm grateful to have the chance to see this, and I hope to get a good look at the truffles themselves when they're harvested.'

Winnow approached as Mel made this statement.

The three princes were all about business after that. It was strange to stand back and watch these three privileged men go about digging bits of fungus out from beneath beds of rotting leaves. Rufusina did her thing, and Rik praised her for being a good hog, at which the pig sort of…preened, Mel thought fancifully, and checked her own feet to make sure they hadn't sprouted those sparkly shoes while she was daydreaming.

'This one looks good, brother. And smell the pungent odour.' Anrai handed a truffle to Rik.

Rik examined the truffle. 'It is good. Take a look at it, Melanie.'

Before Mel could blink, the truffle had been dumped into her hands. She didn't know much about truffles. Not in this state, but that didn't stop her from wanting to cook with them, to discover if they were indeed as fine as it was claimed, to revere the opportunity to hold this piece of life and privilege and history. 'Will they be enough for your marketing plans, Rik?'

She didn't notice the softness in her tone, didn't see the look exchanged between Rik's brothers as Rik bent his shoulders to protect her from the wind that had sprung up as he answered her question.

'I hope so, Mel. I very much hope so.'

They gathered the truffles. Some were sent with Winnow to be prepared for travel. Rik placed the others in a basket, thanked his brothers for their presence and saw them on their way, and then turned to Mel. 'Shall we have that peek at the kitchen that you mentioned?'

'Y-yes. I'd like that.' Mel liked it even more that Rik had remembered that small comment of hers from days ago.

They made their way to the kitchens. Rik introduced Mel to the staff and somehow, even though she'd always been on the other side of things in this environment, he made it comfortable and easy. Enough that when he had to excuse himself to attend to other matters, Mel accepted the invitation to remain behind and observe as the staff prepared the midday meals.

'I'm almost afraid to taste,' Melanie murmured as Rik removed the cover from the last dish.

They were in his suite. He'd asked for their meal to be sent here, and wasn't that what people would expect of a newly engaged couple—to want every moment alone? Yet Rik knew that he'd chosen to dine with Melanie here because *he* wanted to keep her to himself more than he perhaps should.

The legend talked of sharing the first meal prepared with the truffles, that the prince must share the tasting process...

He pushed the fanciful thoughts aside. This was a matter of practicality. And perhaps of giving Melanie a moment that she might not otherwise experience. 'Each of the dishes have been enhanced with the addition of the truffles.'

'The kitchen staff said there are different opinions about actually cooking the truffles.' Mel had listened with interest to the discussion about that in the kitchens earlier. She'd learned so much! 'The risotto and the duck dishes both smell divine.'

'Before we start on those, I would like to give you the chance to sample the first truffle in very simple form.' Rik lifted a single truffle from a salver. His fingers shook slightly. He steadied them and lifted his gaze to hers.

It was just a legend. Foolish stuff.

The prince prepares the truffle and offers it to his bride.

Mel drew a shaky breath as though she perhaps, too, felt the air change around them, almost as though it filled with anticipation as she yielded her palate to his ministration...

He shaved transparent slices of truffle onto the pristine white plate. The butter knife slid through creamy butter. Just the right smear on each sliver, a sprinkle of salt crystals.

Rik held the first slice out to her. Soft pink lips closed over it, just touched the tips of his fingers as her eyelids drifted closed and she experience her first taste of...a legend.

'It's almost intoxicating.' Her words whispered through her lips. 'The permeation of the scent, the beautiful texture. I can't even describe how amazing...I feel as though I've tasted something sacred.'

She couldn't have rehearsed those words if she'd tried. Rik took his own slice of truffle, unbelievably pleased in the face of *her* pleasure.

They moved on to eat the other dishes. Melanie experienced each new taste with curiosity and perhaps with a little awe. Rik shared her pleasure and knew that it renewed his own. He couldn't take his gaze from her mouth. He wanted to lean forward and taste the flavour of the truffle, of salt and butter, from the inside of her lips.

It was just a legend.

But Melanie Watson was not a legend. She was a very real woman, and Rik…desired her in this moment, far too much.

They left for France that afternoon. Mel settled into her seat on the family's private plane and observed, with some wonder, Rik's calm face. 'I don't know how you do it.'

'Do what?' He glanced out of the window at the scudding clouds beneath the plane's belly before he turned his gaze to her and gave her all of his attention.

'Remain so calm in the face of being chased all the way to the plane by a wedding planner waving colour swatches and bits of lace and begging for fittings and a decision on the choices for the table settings.'

'We gave her the answers she needed.' A slight smile twitched at the corners of Rik's mouth. 'And perhaps next time she won't wear those kinds of heels for running.'

'I could learn a thing or two.' Melanie had taken

to the wedding planner. 'She's doing her best to make things easy for us while we fly all over Europe showing buyers what they'll be missing out on if they don't make an order this year for Braston truffles.'

'In truth we're only going to Paris.' There was a pause while Rik looked into her eyes, and while he registered how committed she had sounded to his country's industry as she spoke those words.

'It's still more exciting than almost anything I've done.' Melanie returned his glance.

How did he do that? Make it seem as though the whole rest of the world suddenly faded away and it were just the two of them? Mel would be hopeless at truly being married to him. There'd be photos through the tabloids all the time of her making goo-goo eyes at him when she didn't realise she was doing it.

Um, where was she?

She would not, anyway. An unguarded thought here or there, or coming to realise that he was a good man and one she could admire, hardly equated to a Rufusina-like devotion to the man.

And you just compared yourself to a truffle hog, Mel. I don't think pigs wear magic slippers. 'Magic trotters, maybe,' Mel muttered, and snapped her teeth together before anything even sillier could come out.

'I hope the marketing trip is successful.' For a moment Rik dropped his guard and let her see the concern beneath the surface. 'There's no room for failure in my plans, but I still…'

Worry?

'All the kitchen staff said the truffles were the best

ever. I have nothing to compare to, but I thought they were stunning.' Mel was glad she'd spent the time in the kitchen while Rik finalised plans for their trip.

He'd sprung it on her just as though they were taking a walk around the corner. "Oh, and by the way we're leaving for Paris this afternoon, I'll have the staff pack for you."

She'd let that happen, too, and hadn't even tried to oversee what got put in the suitcases. Melanie Watson, cook, had stayed clear and let the palace staff pack her things for a trip to Paris.

'I'll help you in any way I can, with the marketing efforts.' Mel didn't know if she could do anything. Did being his fiancée count?

Her glance dropped to the ring on her finger. Every time she looked at it, it seemed to belong there more than the last time. It had seemed to be made for her from the moment Rik lifted it from a bed of black velvet and placed it on her finger.

What was happening to her? She was losing the battle to keep her emotional distance from him, that was what. There was no point saying she only cared about the people of Braston, or only admired him because he cared about their futures. Mel did feel all those things, but they were only part of what she felt for him.

Face it, Mel. Somehow you got caught in your own feelings towards him and, instead of getting them under control or stopping them altogether, they've grown more and more with each passing day.

CHAPTER NINE

'I AM interested, you understand. Braston black truffles have been a high-standard product.' The owner of the group of elite Parisian restaurants spoke the words to Rik with a hint of regret, but as much with the glint of good business in his eyes. 'It is just with your truffles being totally off the market for two years I have found other supply sources.'

This was the fourth restaurant owner they'd seen since they arrived in Paris. The others had come on board, but something told Mel this one might be a harder sell.

They were inside the man's home, seated at a carved wooden dining setting. At the end of the table, a wide glass vase held a bunch of mixed flowers. The moment they walked into the room, Rik's gaze had examined the arrangement.

He'd been checking for gardenias, Mel had realised, and her heart had been ridiculously warmed by the gesture on his part. There were none, but that bunch of flowers looked particularly pretty to her now.

'The blight to our crops was tragic, but we are back

on our feet and, as you can see, the commercial truffles are the same high standard.' Rik lifted one of the truffles he had placed on an oval plate in the centre of the table, took up a stainless-steel shaver and shaved thin slices from the black shape.

As the older man examined the truffle slices, and Mel recalled the almost spiritual moment of trying her first truffle with Rik, he went on.

'I know at this time of year you would be sourcing truffles. I'd like to see Braston truffles back on the menu at your restaurants.'

At his feet was a travel carrier containing more truffles, and from which he had unpacked the plates and shaver as well as a beautiful small kitchen knife with a gold inlaid handle.

'And I'd like to put them there, but—'

'I have an added incentive that may sweeten the deal for you, Carel.' Rik spoke the words quietly.

'And that is?' Carel was the last on their list.

It was almost nine p.m. now and they had been fortunate that the man rarely worked in any of his kitchens these days, preferring to visit as suited him, so he'd been more than happy to meet with Rik at his home.

The incentive of the truffles harvested from royal grounds had worked well with the other restaurant owners. They'd all placed orders for commercial truffles so they could also obtain some of the other truffles. Mel wondered if Carel would be as willing to be convinced. Middle-aged, and ruthlessly business focused, this man was much harder to read than the others.

A surge of protectiveness of Rik rose in Mel's breast.

He shouldn't have to beg for anything. He was, well, he was a prince! And yet that description was not the first one that had come to Mel's mind. Rik was good and fair and hardworking and dedicated and his care for the people of his country ran so deep that she knew it would never leave him. He deserved to be respected because of what was inside him.

Carel tipped his head slightly to the side. 'We have already discussed pricing and you certainly do not plan to give away —'

'Braston's truffle crops at a price that won't help my people get back on their feet?' Rik said it softly. 'No. And deep down I know you would not respect such a gesture if I made it.'

The older man was silent for a moment before he dipped his head. 'You are correct.'

'How would you feel about a complimentary gift of some of the truffles grown on the palace grounds?' Rik watched Carel's face for his reaction. 'To go with your order, of course.'

Mel watched both their faces.

'There are legends surrounding those truffles.' The older man's glance moved to Mel before it returned to Rik and he asked with the hint of a smile, 'Do I need to ask whether you harvested the truffles yourself? I am assuming you have brought them with you to show?'

'You do not need to ask, and I have brought them.' Rik's answer was ironic and guarded all at once.

Before Mel could try to understand that, Rik drew another white rectangular plate out and placed just one truffle on it.

Carel leaned forward to look.

Rik shaved the truffle, allowing the wafer thin slices to fall onto the plate and the pungent aroma to rise.

What exactly did that legend stand for? Mel made a note to find out when they got back to the palace.

'The aroma is muscular with a particular rich spiciness I have never encountered.' Carel lifted one of the slices to examine the texture, and colour.

He looked, he inhaled, and after a long moment he put the truffle slice down. 'I do not know. I'm not convinced that the royal truffles will equate to anything exciting enough on the plate. If I agreed to your offer, I would want to be sure that the truffles were a good enough selling point in terms of taste, not only legend.'

'And yet they *are* the stuff of legends,' Rik said with a hint of the same spark.

This was the business dance, and both men were doing it well.

'Indeed.' The older man dipped his head. 'That is undeniable and an excellent marketing point. But I would be using them at my restaurants for the most expensive dishes only on a very limited basis. They would have to live up to and beyond expectation in all ways.'

'They do. They would!' The words burst out of Mel. She touched the edge of one truffle slice with the tip of her finger and caught and held Carel's gaze. 'These truffles have a flavour and scent you'll never find anywhere else. The texture is beautiful. They provide the most stunning enhancement to the dishes they're used in or when eaten by themselves.'

'This is quite true.' Rik's gaze softened as he glanced

at Melanie's face. She wanted so desperately for this trip to be successful, for him to obtain all the markets for his truffles that he had set out to recapture. 'But I understand Carel's point, too.'

Rik appreciated Mel for that investment in him. It seemed a bland way to describe the warm feeling that spread through his chest as he acknowledged Melanie's fierce support of his efforts. It *was* a bland description, but Rik wasn't at all sure he wanted to allow himself to examine that warmth, or try to know exactly what it might mean.

'For me, I do not have the evidence of this truth.' Carel again smelled and examined the truffle and its slices. 'I am sure my chefs would like to try cooking with these, but they are busy at the restaurants—'

'*I'll* cook them for you!' Melanie got out of her chair. 'Right here and now.'

If Carel had given any indication that he wouldn't allow it, no doubt Melanie would have immediately stopped. But the older man simply watched with a hint of appreciation on his face as Melanie fired up on Rik's behalf. Carel waved a hand as though to say: By all means go ahead.

Rik had to push back a bite of possessive jealousy as he realised the older man was…aware of his fiancée as a woman.

Surely this doesn't surprise you, Rik? Every man would notice her beauty. How could they not?

Melanie stepped into Carel's open-plan kitchen. It was immediately apparent that she was at home in this environment. A chopping board sat on the bench.

She glanced towards the refrigerator. 'May I use anything, *monsieur*?'

Carel smiled. 'Yes. Anything.'

Mel took chicken breast, salad greens and dried raspberries, and then selected a bottle of red wine. Finally she retrieved salt and pepper and cashews and a long thin loaf of bread from Carel's pantry.

Rather than the kitchen knives available to her, Mel walked back to where Rik sat at the table. She took the gold-handled knife from where it rested near Rik's right hand.

As she did so she touched his shoulder briefly with her other hand. 'For luck.'

He didn't know whether she meant the knife, or the touch. Perhaps both.

'Your fiancée has pluck.' The Frenchman spoke the words quietly as he sat back to watch Melanie take control of his kitchen. 'I shall eagerly observe this.'

A half-hour later, Mel drew a deep breath and carried the chicken salad to the table. The meal looked good on the plate, colourful and versatile, full of different textures with the thin slices of truffle heated through and releasing their gorgeous aroma. The wine reduction made a beautiful sauce. The thick slice of bread coated with beaten egg yolk, the lightest combination of chopped herbs and grated sharp cheese and lightly toasted made a perfect accompaniment.

Even so, the proof would be in the taste, not only the visual appeal. Mel placed the dish before her host and brought the other two servings for Rik and herself.

Minutes later, Carel put down fork and knife and

lifted his gaze. He spoke first to Rik. 'The truffles are better than anything I have ever tasted. Cooked in the right way, and served with a little royal legendary on the side, these will be highly sought after at my restaurants this season. I am happy to place my order with you.'

'Thank you.' Rik dipped his head and cast a smile in Mel's direction. 'And thanks to you, Melanie, for this meal. You are a wonder in the kitchen. I did not realise just how skilled you are.'

'I would have you in any of my kitchens, Melanie.' Carel's statement followed Rik's.

And while Mel basked in Rik's surprise and the fact that he'd obviously enjoyed the meal, she had to be judicious about it. 'I have to confess that I watched the truffles being prepared at the palace today and learned all I could from the process.'

She turned to smile at the Frenchman. 'Thank you for your compliment.'

'In truth it is a job offer.' The man's gaze shifted between Mel and Rik. 'Any of my restaurants, any time. Permanent work, good wages and conditions. You would be more than welcome. Not that I suggest you would be available…'

Mel was more "available" than the man realised. She said something that she hoped was appropriately appreciative but non-committal. Carel didn't know that she and Rik wouldn't remain together as a couple, so she couldn't exactly have asked the man to hold that thought for a few months.

Plus there'd be work permits and all sorts of things, and when this was all over Mel would need to be back

in Australia. She tried valiantly not to let those thoughts
spread a pall over Carel's acceptance. Conversation
moved on then. Mel sat back and let Rik lead those topics with their host. And *she* tried to gather her calm, and
not think too much about the future. Not tonight. Not
here in Paris. Not while she felt…vulnerable in this way.

'I hope you will excuse us if we leave you now,' Rik
said twenty minutes later.

They had shared a second glass of wine with Carel
but it was getting late. 'It is time for us to return to our
hotel.' He thanked the man again for his business, and
then he and Melanie were outside.

'I would like to stroll the streets before we go back
to our hotel.' He turned to examine her face. 'Are you
up to a walk?'

'That would be…I would like that.' Her response
was guarded. She hoped he couldn't hear that within
her words. Beneath it there was too much delight, and
that made her feel vulnerable. 'I'd like to see a little
more of P-Paris by night.'

'Then I will get our driver to drop us a few blocks
away from our hotel.' Rik did this, and they made their
car trip in silence before they got out to walk the rest
of the way.

The hotel Dominico had booked for Rik was in a
beautiful part of the city. At first Melanie felt a little stilted with Rik, but he linked his arm with hers
and told her the history of the area, pointing out buildings. And using the night and this moment to enjoy
her closeness?

Dream on, Melanie Watson!

'I never thought I would see places like Paris, and Braston.' Melanie turned her face to look into his. 'It's very beautiful on your side of the world.'

'It is…' His gaze seemed to linger on her eyes, her mouth, before he turned his glance back to the buildings around them. 'We have some time in the morning. Is there something you'd like to do?'

'I would love to see some markets.' Mel tried to keep her enthusiasm at a reasonable level. She did. But the chance to explore Paris, even a small portion of it. How could she not be excited? 'A peek at some local colour?'

'Then we shall find markets tomorrow,' Rik said and tucked her more closely against his side. For a moment he felt, not resistance, but perhaps her effort to maintain what she considered to be an appropriate mental and emotional distance?

He should resist, too, but tonight…he did not want to. And so he walked calmly until he felt her relax against his side, and then he took the pleasure of these moments with her in peace, away from expectations and work commitments and other things that went with being… who he was.

'I am enjoying being anonymous with you right now, Melanie.' His voice deepened on the words, on the confession. He couldn't hold the words back.

'Sometimes I forget that you're a prince.' She almost whispered the words in response, as though they were a guilty secret. 'You make extraordinary things seem everyday and normal. Then I forget who you are and just—' She broke off.

Treated him as a man?

Dangerous territory, Rik. The next step is to believe she likes you purely because of you and not your title, and then there would be a woman seeing the man first.

If Rik allowed himself to form any kind of attachment to that woman it could be difficult to let her go when the time came.

He had to do that, and he had no proof that she liked him in any way particularly. Other than kisses, and could he really say those kisses meant all of these things?

You don't have the faith to look for anything else. You've allowed your upbringing to taint your outlook, to stunt what you will reach out for.

In an attempt to refocus his thoughts, he turned his attention back to their visit to Carel. 'You said you'd been a cook, but I did not know you had such skills as you displayed tonight. You won Carel over to placing that order.'

Rik's compliments warmed Mel. 'I enjoyed cooking with the truffles tonight, and I'm so relieved that Carel liked the dish. I took a risk. I wondered if you might have felt I stepped out of line.'

Mel searched his face. 'I—I could just as easily have *lost* you that deal!'

'I do not think so.' Rik gave a slight shake of his head. 'He was too enamoured of you from the first moment. The job offer he made…'

'Was flattering but it's out of the question, isn't it?' She didn't make a question out of it. Well, it wasn't one! 'I've signed on to help you, not to try to set myself up to cook in a Paris restaurant the day after our m-marriage ends.' Mel crossed her fingers and prayed that Rik hadn't heard that slight stumble when she'd referred to that last bit.

'You are very faithful, Nicole Melanie Watson.' Rik shifted his arm and instead caught her hand in his.

His fingers were strong and warm and familiar, and Mel couldn't stop from curling hers around them.

Rik's eyes softened as he smiled at her. 'That is rare and I admire you for it very much.'

They continued their walk in silence, just strolling side by side as though they had all the time in the world. As though they didn't have a *care* in the world.

But underneath, tensions simmered. If everything were so comfortable and unthreatening, why did Mel's heart beat faster with each step they took? Why did a sense of hope and anticipation mix with her awareness of Rik and make her want their walk never to end, and yet at the same time make her want to return to the hotel because she hoped against hope...

That he would kiss her goodnight again? That this night would never end? That it would end for her in his arms? All such foolish thoughts!

'Here we are.' Perhaps he felt it, too, because he swept her into the hotel without another word.

And it seemed as though time warped then because they were at the door of their suite before she could draw a breath, and yet she remembered the endless silent moments in the lift, just the two of them, wishing she could reach out to him, wishing she had the right...

Face it, Mel. You're starting to care for him. To care

for Prince Rikardo Ettonbierre of Braston. Caring as though you might be…

Caring for a man who was a good man, but also a prince, and that meant he was not any man for her because she was an everyday girl.

Mel didn't know what she was thinking, what she hoped for!

Except for a kiss from…a prince?

No. A kiss from Rikardo. That was what she wanted and needed. He *was* a prince, but he could have been the boy next door and she would have wanted that kiss just as much.

You are in trouble, Mel. Big, big trouble because you can't fall for him!

The scent of brewed coffee met them as they entered the suite. A glass bowl with fruits, a bottle of wine and chocolates sat on the low coffee table near the sofa and chairs, and, in the small kitchenette, a basket held fresh baked croissants. The lights were turned down. The suite looked ready to welcome lovers.

Mel's breath caught in the back of her throat. They weren't, of course. There were two bedrooms. It wasn't as though she and Rik—

'The coffee smells good. Just the ticket after that walk in the night air.' Mel stripped off her coat and followed her nose to the kitchenette. She felt she did really well at acting completely normal and unconcerned.

Except she should have dodged the idea of coffee altogether, said goodnight and headed straight for her room rather than prolonging this. What if Rik thought she'd done that so they could take advantage of this romantic scene? What if he thought she was angling for more of his company for that reason?

'You don't need to have any, of course,' she blurted, and then added, because that could have been taken as rather ungracious, 'but I'll pour you a cup if you like, and if you're hungry I can get you a croissant.'

'Coffee would be welcome.' He briefly glanced at the food items and away again. 'I do not think I will spoil the memory of that meal just now.'

Mel found two cups. She got them out of the cupboard and filled them with steaming liquid, and was proud that her fingers didn't tremble.

There was an enclosed balcony, beautifully warm and secluded with stunning views. They took their drinks out there and stood side by side soaking in the ambiance of the city lights.

They weren't touching and yet Mel felt so close to him, so aware of him. How was she supposed to walk away at the end of this arrangement without…looking back and wishing?

If wishes were horses then beggars would ride. Wasn't that the saying? She wasn't a beggar, but she was also not the princess who lived around the corner from the prince. She and Rik weren't on an even playing field; they never would be. Mel needed to remember that. She had to remember who he was, and who she was.

'I am pleased with this evening's efforts.' Rik set his empty coffee cup down on the ledge, took hers and placed it beside it. 'I've regained four key markets.

There are others to chase but those are smaller and can be done out of Braston over the next couple of weeks.'

'You've taken a big step towards getting the people back on their financial feet.' There was pride in her voice that she couldn't hide. In the soft night light Mel looked into his face and knew that her happiness for him must show. 'You've earned the right to feel some peace.'

'You have played a part in my peace.' He spoke softly, with a hint of discovery and perhaps acceptance in his voice. 'And I should keep my distance from you. I know it, but I do not want to do it.'

Her breath quivered in her throat. 'What is it that you want to do?'

'This.' Rik leaned in and claimed her lips with his.

'Melanie.' Rik breathed her name into her hair. Her face was pressed against his chest. He had kissed her until they were both breathless with it. He wanted to kiss her again, and with his fingertips he gently raised her chin.

Her eyes glowed, filled with softness and passion for him. She'd told him there were times when she had thought of him as a man, not a prince. Rik wanted that acceptance from her now, for her to see him as Rikardo, regardless of what else there might be in his life. For once he simply wanted to be a man to a woman.

He drew her soft curves more securely into his arms and breathed the scent from the side of her neck and let his mouth cover hers once again. Tongues caressed and a low moan sounded. His, and a warning bell began to register in the back of his mind not to do this because there was naivety in the way she yielded to him, as though she was new to this, as though perhaps she wasn't particularly experienced...

'What are we doing?' Melanie spoke in a low tone. She drew back. Shields rose in her eyes, concealing her reaction to him, protecting her. 'This—this isn't the same as before when there was a reason to kiss me. It doesn't matter about Paris, about the romance of being here. I shouldn't have let myself be tempted. I shouldn't have looked for that—'

Her words were disjointed. Discomfort filled her face, and Rik...wished it didn't have to be that way, but hadn't he set them up for exactly this? He'd made his choices. 'I should not have stepped over this line, either. It was not a smart thing to do.'

He wrestled with his own reactions. He'd wanted to take, conquer, claim—to stamp his ownership on her and possess her until she was his and his alone. That urge had bypassed all his usual roadblocks.

'I have never—' He stopped himself from completing the sentence. Instead he tried to turn his attention to tomorrow. 'You must go to bed now, get some sleep ready for our visit to the markets.'

Her eyes still held the glaze of the moments of passion they had shared, but they also held confusion, uncertainty, and unease. She searched his face and Rik saw each emotion register as she found her way back to here and now and...to who they were and to remembrance of the arrangement they shared. *He* should have never forgotten that arrangement, yet when he was near her he couldn't seem to remember even the most basic of principles, of sticking to his word and to their goals.

'Thank you for showing me a little of Paris this evening, and for allowing me to take part in your talks with the restaurateurs.' Her chin tipped up. 'Goodnight, Rikardo. I hope you sleep well.'

CHAPTER TEN

'THANK you for finding these markets for me to see.' Mel let her gaze shift from one market stall to the next as she and Rik walked through them. Somehow that felt much easier than looking the prince in the eyes.

They'd kissed last night and she'd withdrawn. Did he know how far she had stepped over the line within herself by entering into that kiss? Mel was too close to falling dangerously for…a prince. She couldn't do that. She had to be businesslike about her relationship with Rik, even if their surroundings or circumstances felt very romantic or extraordinary.

No matter what, Mel. You have to keep your distance inside yourself no matter what. So treat this outing as an outing. Nothing more and nothing less.

She drew a breath and forced her gaze to his. 'Thank you for making time for us to come here.'

'You are welcome, Melanie.' His tone, too, sounded more formal than usual.

And were his shoulders held a little more rigidly?

Mel tried very hard after that, to focus only on the moment. The markets were a treasure trove of local clothing, some new, brand name and quite expensive but with equally much vintage and pre-loved. It was the latter that appealed to Mel.

'You are sure you don't want to look at the branded items?' When they arrived here Rik had pressed what felt like a very large bundle of currency into Mel's hands, and instructed her that she was not to leave empty-handed.

That, too, had felt awkward. Ironically, not because he had wanted to give her this gift but because they had both let their fingers linger just a little too long, and then quickly withdrawn.

Mel's thoughts started to whirl as they had last night in the long hours of courting sleep that wouldn't come. A part of her wanted to find a way to get him to care for her truly. *That* was the problem.

He didn't, and he wouldn't. Not today, not tomorrow or next week or next month or in any number of months. At the end of their time together he would send her away from him fully. How much more did she need to think about it before she accepted that fact? Accepted that a few kisses in the heat of the moment in a beautiful city didn't mean all that much to a man who could kiss just about anyone, anywhere and any time?

Mel drew a slow breath. She forced air into her lungs, forced calm into her inner turmoil. And she cast her glance once more about the market and kept looking until the blur of colours turned once again into garments piled on tables, and she spotted a pretty skirt and moved closer to look…

'I'd like to buy this one.' It wouldn't break the bank.

In fact, it was ridiculously cheap. But it was exactly what Mel would wear, a long, beautifully warm tan suede that fell in an A-line cut. A memento of Paris. That thought, too, was bittersweet. 'It should fit me, but even if it doesn't I can take it in.'

She held out the rest of the money. 'Thank you for giving me this gift. I'd like to browse a little longer and then I'll be ready to go.' She hoped her words were convincing and didn't sound as strained as she felt.

'You must keep that to spend any time you wish.' Rik pressed the money back into her hands, and waited for her to tuck it away in her purse.

As the days passed after Paris, Melanie showed her strength by being the perfect fiancée to Rik. No one, not his brothers and not his father, could have said that she wasn't fully supportive of him, utterly committed to him.

Not in love with him, perhaps. That kind of acting would be a stretch, but the rest yes. She maintained her role beautifully. She showed no stress. She seemed perfectly content as she forged ahead making plans for their marriage, liaising with all those involved in the preparations as the days slid closer to the first of the three wedding rehearsals. But beneath the surface...

Rik was not content. He couldn't forget holding her in his arms in Paris. He, who had grown up trained to live by his self-control, had felt that night as though he teetered on the brink of losing it. He had longed, *longed deep down inside*, to make love to her but Melanie had broken away.

'You behaved like some smitten, lovelorn—' He bit the words off before he added fiancé. It was already bad enough that he was talking to the walls as he walked along. He *was* Melanie's fiancé. Just not in any normal sense of the word.

Their first rehearsal was tomorrow and he did not feel prepared. Perhaps things were just moving too quickly for his comfort, for him to feel that he possessed that control that he needed to have. All would be safe in Melanie's capable hands. Instinctively he knew this. Provided the actual marriage day went ahead, anything else would not overly matter anyway...

Rik made his way to the kitchen. The palace always had kitchen staff on call. He could have got one out of bed to make him a cup of coffee or a sandwich or to bring him pickings from the refrigerators, but he would rather forage for himself. At least it would pass some time until he managed to nod off, and Mel would be safe and sound asleep in *her* bed while Rik wrestled his demons.

That was part of his insomnia problem, knowing Mel was so close and he couldn't touch her. Mustn't touch her. He strode to the double doors of the palace kitchen and pushed with both hands. Before he even opened them, the scent of fresh baking hit him.

Why would anyone be baking at this time of night? Baking up a storm, he realised as his gaze lit on an array of cakes and cookies spread on the bench.

Something tickled the back of his mind, and was lost as he realised *who* was doing the cooking. 'Mel—'

'Rik! Oh, you startled me.' The cake plate she held

in her hands bobbled before she carefully set it down and placed a lid over it.

'I had permission.' Her words were almost defensive. 'I needed some time in the kitchen. It's what I do when I need—' She cut the words off, waved a hand. 'Well, never mind. I'm almost done here, anyway. All I need to do is leave the kitchen sparkling. It's almost there now.' Mel turned to wipe down a final bench top.

She had dark smudges under her eyes. Was Melanie, too, more disturbed than he'd realised since their trip to Paris despite her valiant efforts to support him? Was she also feeling tortured and struggling with her thoughts?

Leave the cleaning up for the staff.

Rik wanted very much to say the words. He bit them back because it seemed important to her to leave the kitchen as she had found it. Aside from those cakes and cookies.

'The staff told me these could be used tomorrow.' Mel gestured towards the food items. She went on to mention some need for the foods.

Rik only half heard the explanation, because he was looking at those smudges beneath her eyes.

'I don't suppose you're hungry?' She gestured towards a chocolate cake covered in sticky icing. 'It's probably the worst thing to do, but I thought I'd eat a piece and maybe—'

'Relax for a while?' He didn't know what she'd planned to say, but to Rik, standing in the kitchen in the middle of the night unable to sleep, with Melanie obviously also unable to sleep, it made perfect sense to use his insomnia to try to at least help *her* to relax. 'Why don't we take it back with us?'

Mel hadn't expected Rik to walk in on her cooking splurge. He was the reason for it, so maybe it would be good to spend that time with him. Perhaps then she would be able to shake off the feeling of melancholy and impending loss that had become harder and harder to bear as each day passed.

You'd better smile anyway, Mel. He doesn't need to see your face and start wondering what your problem is.

In truth Mel didn't *know* what the problem was. She'd hoped that cooking would shake the answer loose but it hadn't.

'I guess we can make coffee in our suite?' It was only after she said the words that she realised she'd referred to the suite as theirs as though she had every right, as though she had as much ownership of it as Rik did.

'I put a pot on before I left.'

His words made her realise that, while he'd caught her cooking in the middle of the night because she couldn't sleep, he must have had similar problems otherwise he wouldn't have been wandering the corridors and making pots of coffee when normal people would be asleep in their beds.

Mel put pieces of cake onto plates and loaded them onto a tray, which Rik promptly took from her hands. One final glance around the kitchen showed that the staff would have nothing more to deal with than delivering the goodies tomorrow morning, and Mel would try to be available to help with that.

The smell of brewed coffee met them as they stepped into the suite. It reminded Mel of Paris, of being held in his arms and kissed.

'Did the suede skirt fit, or did you have to alter it?' Rik's words made Mel realise that he, too, was remembering.

Her breath hitched for a moment. She forced her thoughts away from the reaction. She'd got through day after day doing the same. Each time any unacceptable thought tried to raise its head, Mel pushed it away. Surely no one would be able to tell just how often she thought about Rik, about those moments? How she longed for them all over again? 'The skirt fits perfectly. I'm planning to wear it tomorrow, actually.'

For the festival being held in the town. Rik hadn't spoken of it, so Mel didn't know what his role of involvement would be, if any. And the kitchen staff had told her that the event itself would be a low budget affair.

That didn't mean it couldn't be fun, though, and it was an unusual theme. Mel at least wanted to take a look. All of which was trivia, really, and yet there were times when trivia felt a little less emotionally threatening than the rest of life!

They sat side by side on the sofa eating cake and sipping coffee. A very ordinary, normal thing to do except for the fact it was after midnight, and this was Rik's suite of rooms, and they were engaged and yet in the truest sense they really weren't.

She blurted out, 'The wedding planner supervised

a fitting of the gown this afternoon. I won't wear it to
the first rehearsal tomorrow, of course, but…'

How did she explain what she couldn't understand
herself? Just how much that fitting had taken from her
emotionally and she couldn't say why because it was
just a dress in the end, and the wedding wasn't going
to be real, and Mel *knew* all of this.

Mel didn't want to think about why. 'Well, it's a beautiful gown. I'm amazed at how quickly it's being created.' She drew a breath and tried to make light of it
as she went on. 'Have you been fitted for your suit?'

'Yesterday.' He glanced towards her. 'I've left you
to handle the bulk of the work for this wedding while I
attended to other things. I should have supported you
better.'

She leaned towards him, shook her head. 'You've
been all over the country checking on the truffle harvesting, making sure the orders are going out in perfect
condition. That's so important.'

'And that's your generosity shining again.' He lifted
his hand to the side of her face. 'You have a tiny dot
of cake batter right there.' His fingertip softly brushed
the spot.

Mel closed her eyes. Oh, it was the stupidest thing
to do but it was what his touch did to her. She melted
any time they were close.

'It's there, isn't it?' The feather-light touch of lips
replaced his fingertip against her cheek. He kissed the
spot where her cooking efforts had made their way
onto her face, and then he sighed softly and pressed

his cheek to hers. 'All the time that need is there. I do not know why.'

That was as far as he got, because he turned his head to look into her eyes, and Mel turned her head to look into his eyes, and their lips met.

The fire ignited. Immediately and utterly and Rik's arms closed around her and Mel threw hers around his neck and held on. She didn't know if she could have let go if she'd wanted to. This was what had been troubling her. This was what she'd tried to think about and figure out.

Her thoughts formed that far, and then they became action. Her mouth yielded to his, opened to him even as she took from him. She sipped from his lips and ran her tongue across his teeth.

Everything was pleasure, and somehow all of those feelings seemed to have caught themselves in a place deep in her chest where they swirled and twined and warmed her all at once. Rik was the warming power. Everything about him drew her. Mel didn't want to resist being drawn.

'I don't want to leave this, Mel.' His words echoed her thoughts, and he used the diminutive of her name, and Mel loved that.

'I don't want to leave it, either, Rik.'

'Do you understand what will happen?' His words were very deep, emotive and desirous and almost stern all at once.

'I do.' If there was any hesitation in her words it was not because of uncertainty in that decision. 'This—this is new for me.'

Please don't stop because I've admitted that.

'But it's what I want, Rik. I—I have no doubts.'

'I do not want to consider doubts, either.' Rik's words were strong, and yet the touch of his hand was so gentle as he stroked the side of her face, her neck. 'I will cherish you, Melanie. I will cherish you through this experience.'

That made it right for her. It just…did. The tiny bit of fear that had been buried deep down, that she might not know what to do or how to please him, evaporated. He would guide her. Mel could give this gift and share the gift of his intimacy in return. She wanted that. She *needed* it, though she did not understand why that need held such strength.

Rik took her hand and led her to his bedroom. Mel managed to register that the room was similar to her own but with a more manly tone, and then Rik drew her into his arms and kissed his way from the side of her neck to her chin and finally to her lips as their bodies pressed together and Mel didn't notice anything more about the room.

This felt exactly right. That was what Mel thought as her hands pressed against his chest, slid up to his shoulders and she let herself touch his muscular back through the cloth of his shirt. Yet that was not enough. 'I want—'

'What do you want, Melanie? Tell me.' He encouraged her to put her need into words.

And maybe he needed to hear that, too, for her to tell him.

'I need to touch you. I need to feel your skin beneath my fingertips while you're kissing me.' She almost whispered it, but he heard and he guided her hand to the buttons of his shirt.

It was all the permission that Mel needed, and, though she trembled inside, her fingers slipped each button free until his chest was revealed and she could touch his bare skin. 'You're so warm.'

'That is because you are in my arms.' He shrugged out of the shirt and then he gave all of his attention to her and to this exploration that they shared moment-by-moment in giving and receiving and discovering and finding.

When he laid her on the bed, Mel looked into his eyes and though her thoughts and feelings were blurred by passion, impossible to define, every instinct told her. 'This is what I've needed. I know it's right. I want you to make love to me, Rik. Just to share this together, the two of us without thinking about anything else.'

Rik cupped her face in his palm. 'And so it will be.'

Melanie blossomed beneath Rik's ministrations. She was beautiful in every way, and he told her in English and French and told her in the old language of Braston, words that he had never uttered to another woman as he led her forward on this journey.

He hesitated on the brink of claiming her. 'I am sorry that there will be pain. If you want me to stop—'

'No.' Mel let the word be a caress of her lips against his. A sigh inside her. A whisper of need that she gave from her heart, and that was terrifying because Mel couldn't bring her heart to this. That was far too dangerous a thing to do. 'Please don't stop, Rik. I...don't think I could bear it if you did.'

There *was* pain, but she held his gaze and the tenderness in his eyes, the expression that seemed akin to awe as he bent to kiss her lips again, allowed her to release that pain, to let it pass and to trust in him to lead her forward.

He did that, and then there was only pleasure and she crashed suddenly over an incredible wave and he cried out with her, the most amazing experience Mel had ever experienced, and the most powerful, knowing that she, too, had brought *him* to *this*.

Afterwards he held her cuddled against his chest as their breathing slowed. A deep lethargy crept up on Mel. She tried to fight it, to stay alert, to even *begin* to figure out what happened now or what she should say or do. There was so much and she didn't know how to find understanding but she knew she didn't regret this, could never regret it.

But what did it mean to him, Mel? What did it mean to Rik? Is there any possibility now—?

Mel could have been embarrassed, but they had shared this. How could she now feel anything that even resembled such an emotion? There was no room inside her. She was filled with other emotions, inexplicable to her right now, and overwhelming because what they had shared had been overwhelming. She shivered, wishing for his warmth, and then he was there, drawing her close.

He tucked her chin into his chest and she felt tension

drain from him, too, and wondered what his thoughts might be.

'Sleep, Melanie. You need it right now more than you know.' He stroked his fingers through her hair.

Mel slept.

CHAPTER ELEVEN

'IF I'D remembered this festival was on today I'd have left the country.' Marcelo's face pulled into a disgruntled twist.

'Oh, I don't know. Is it so horrible having the opportunity to flirt with lots of lovely local women?' Anrai dug his brother in the ribs.

Marcelo didn't crack a smile. 'It is if they then want to marry you!'

Anrai, too, now grimaced. 'I forgot that from last year.'

'And the year before and year before and year before,' Marcelo said beneath his breath. 'You need to stop being such a flirt, Anrai. It will catch up with you one day. Anyway, we had to be here. Rik's first wedding rehearsal is later today.' Marcelo turned to Rik. 'Can you believe the marriage is only a week away?'

'No.' Rik glanced at his brothers, heard the sibling teasing. He might even have wanted to join in, if there'd been any space left in his thoughts or emotions right now for anything other than the woman he'd held in his arms last night.

It was just one week before their marriage.

They had spent just one night in each other's arms.

He should not have let that happen but it had and now he did not know what to do, how to go forward. So many thoughts and emotions swirled, and Rik…did not like to feel out of control, confused, uncertain of his path and yet all he could do was continue because… nothing had changed when in a way…everything had. But nothing at the core of him, nothing of how he was. Of his parents' traits within him.

Nevertheless, Rik needed to find Melanie. The marriage *was* only a week away. They did have a rehearsal this afternoon and…he didn't know if he had irreparably messed things up with Melanie.

And even now you wish you could take her again into your arms.

Rik tried to force the thoughts aside. They were of no use to him, a line crossed that must not be crossed again. He glanced around him. He and his brothers were in Ettonbierre village, and, yes, there was a festival on today.

Rik had forgotten all about it. So had Anrai and Marcelo who'd both only arrived back at the palace late last night and had walked out with him this morning intending to meet a man to discuss tourism plans for the region.

All three brothers had plans and goals. All three relied on the success of each other to allow them to achieve those goals. The prize was recovery for a struggling country, the cost to be their freedom if Anrai and

Marcelo could not also figure out ways to avoid their father's insistence that they lock into lifetime marriages.

Rik tried to dismiss the thoughts. He looked around him. This festival was what Melanie had cooked for in the middle of the night. Just a few hours ago, and then Rik had found her in the kitchen and taken her back to his suite. She'd mentioned the wedding rehearsal. She had probably been worrying about it and that had prompted her cooking spree. And then perhaps other thoughts had pushed those worries aside for a time as they…made love.

And those thoughts had now given her new concerns? Of course they would have. They had given Rik fresh concerns, fresh questions. He had to keep her with him and keep both of them to their agreement. He hoped last night would not have undermined that goal. That was the only *clear* path Rik could define. Surely the only one that mattered, so why did reminding himself bring a sense of loss rather than the sense of eventual freedom it should?

Every thought brought Rik back to the same thing. He and Melanie had made love. That *had* changed things. He'd felt as though his world had shifted alignment and Rik couldn't figure out why he felt that way or what it meant.

He'd woken at dawn with Melanie curled in his arms and a sense of rightness that had quickly changed when the reality of what they had done stabbed him in the chest.

How could that have been a smart decision on his part? Melanie had been innocent and had allowed passion to sway her judgement, but Rik was experienced and should have known not to let this happen.

Not when there was no future for them, no future when their involvement was based on a situation that he had set up to avoid becoming tied down in a relationship. He couldn't bear to perpetuate his family's emotional freeze-out into another generation, to be the one turning the cold shoulder to his partner and receiving the same in return. To have his children asking themselves why they were not fit to be loved.

No. He could not carry that legacy forward.

When he woke this morning and thought of all that, remorse and confusion and a lot of other emotions had set in. Melanie was a giving girl. She would be kind. She would definitely care for her children.

But Rik…could not match those traits. He'd eased away from Melanie and got up. Showered, dressed, told himself he needed to think and that he would wait for her to wake and then they would…

What? Somehow sort themselves out so that last night didn't have the impact on them that it already had done?

She'd been a virgin. She'd given him a beautiful gift. That could never be undone now and even with all his concerns, Rik felt that he *had* been given that beautiful gift, the gift of Melanie in all of who she was, and he didn't begin to know what to do now because he hadn't planned for this and he had nothing to give in return of equal or acceptable value.

A confronting thought for a man who always set out to be in charge of his world, who had been raised into position and privilege and must now acknowledge that in this, he lacked.

'I just want to find Melanie.' He frowned. 'There are a lot of people around. She is the fiancée of a prince now, and shouldn't be unattended without at least two bodyguards with her.'

Rik totally overlooked the fact that he had encouraged Melanie to move about the palace grounds and surrounds using the small buggy vehicle, and had believed she would be perfectly safe where members of the palace staff would never be too far away or the villagers would know she was a guest at the palace.

But the festival would bring tourists and strangers. Anything might happen.

And your protectiveness of her is out of proportion to your ability to let her into the core parts of you that you withhold from the world.

But not from his brothers?

That was different. It was all that he had. Care for his brothers and for the people of Braston. He could not bring normal love and caring feelings to a marriage.

'Hate to point it out to you, brother, but *we* don't have any bodyguards with us.' Anrai raised his brows. 'You're sounding very serious considering the temporary nature of your arrangement with Melanie. Much as I think she's a wonderful girl,' his brother added.

'She is.' Rik didn't notice the tightening of his mouth as he spoke, the flash of warring emotions that quickly crossed his face. Instead his gaze scanned the crowds, searching as he missed the surprised and thoughtful gazes his brothers exchanged before they gave nods of silent decision, told him they needed to find their contact and get on with their meeting, and gave him the space to make his search.

Rik glanced around the crowded village square. There were colourful rides for children to play on, stalls out in the open selling home produce and hand-sewn items. A kissing booth, another to have your romantic future read, another for chemistry tests to find potential matches.

The fair had started out as a proposal day centuries ago as a means for men to woo their potential brides with offers of a fowl or a pig as a dowry. Today it had turned into an opportunity for the folk of Ettonbierre village to let their hair down for a day, for children to play and young men and women to flirt with each other, ask each other out.

He didn't want Melanie anywhere near this.

The jealous, protective thought came from deep within Rik. He had no right to it but still it came. A moment later he spotted her and he strode towards the small group gathered outside the food marquee at the edge of the town square.

'It's very flattering of you to say that to me, and yes I guess it would be fair to say that I am a guest of Prince Rikardo at the palace at the moment.' Mel spoke the words as she tried to edge away from the small crowd that had gathered outside the food tent.

She tried to sound normal, polite and not as deeply confused and overwrought as she felt this morning. Pretending calm until she started to feel it was a method that had worked for her after their trip to Paris. Surely it would work again now?

After Paris you were recovering from a kiss. Last night you made love with Rik. The two aren't exactly on a par. 'I'm really not at liberty to discuss that any further at this time.'

Though Rik had assured her none of the villagers would recognise the ring she wore as her engagement ring, Mel tucked her hand into her skirt pocket just in case, and was proud that she'd managed to think clearly enough to consider that need.

In that same thrust to find some sliver of normalcy in the whirl of her emotions she'd delivered all the cakes she could carry to the fair. She had stepped outside the catering tent intending to take a quick look at the festival before heading back to the palace.

Rik had been out on the grounds somewhere when she had first woken up. She probably could have gone looking for him, but what would she have said? She'd needed a moment to try to clear her head before she faced him.

You wanted more than a moment. After all that you shared with him last night you had no idea how to face him. Why downplay it, Mel, when it's all you can think about and every time you do think about it, you can hardly breathe for the mix of feelings that rushes through you?

She'd fallen asleep in his arms, more drained emotionally and in every way than she had understood. And had woken alone, only to realise she was not alone because doubt had come to rest on her shoulder to whisper in her ear. Doubt about his feelings in all of this. Doubt that she had any right to expect him to *have* any feelings about it. Just above the other shoulder lurked despair. Mel didn't want to acknowledge that, but...

She and Rik had shared something. It had been stunningly special to Mel, but that didn't mean it had been any of that to Rikardo. To the prince. How could it have been?

You managed to forget that little factor last night, didn't you? That he's a prince and you're a cook and his path is carefully set and doesn't include any kind of emotional commitment to you.

'If you change your mind while you are here...' The man in front of her gave an engaging smile and handed her a piece of paper with his phone number on it.

Proposal Day. The festival had a history. Mel had heard it all from the kitchen staff. But nowadays it was a chance for people to get to know each other, date or whatever. Mel wouldn't have been interested before. Now that she'd made love with Rik, she felt she could never be interested in any other man, ever again.

The man turned away. There were two others. Mel managed to quickly send them both on their way. She needed to get out of here, to make her way back to the palace and maybe during that solitary walk she would gather up all the pieces of herself and get them back into some kind of working order. Maybe she could hole up in her room for the entire day to complete that task. Would that be long enough?

It will never be long enough, Mel. You know what's happened.

The thought was so strong, so full of conviction. It forced her hand, and realisation crashed over her, then, whether she was ready for it or not.

She'd fallen in love with Rik. It was the answer to why last night had moved her emotions so deeply that she had wondered if she would ever be the same. The answer was no, she never would.

Because "everyday girl" Melanie Watson had fallen in love with Prince Rikardo Ettonbierre of Braston.

It should have been a moment of wonder, of anticipation and happiness. Instead, devastating loss swept through her because last night had been the total of any chance to show her love to him in that way. A moment that shouldn't have happened.

In return, Rik had made no promises. Not at the start of their marriage agreement, and not last night. He'd given in to desire. That wasn't the same as being bowled over by love so that expressing those feelings was imperative.

Mel was the one who had foolishly given her heart. Well, now she had to get back on her feet somehow. She had to get through marrying him and walking away, to do all that with dignity when all she would want to do was beg him to keep her, to want her, to not reject her or abandon her or punish her for—

What did she mean, punish?

And today there was the first wedding rehearsal. How could she get through that?

'Melanie. What are you doing here? Why were you talking to those men?'

Rik's words shook her out of her reverie, stopped

a train of thought that had started to dig into a place deep down where she had hidden parts of herself. But the interruption did not save her from her sense of uncertainty and panic. That increased.

She glanced at him. Oh, it was hard to look and to know what was in her heart.

Please don't let him see it.

That one glance into his face showed austerity, as though he had stepped behind shields, had taken a fortified position.

In that moment he really resembled his father...

Rik had told her he couldn't buy into a cold relationship. He'd been so against the institution of marriage. He...hadn't believed in love.

Mel had thought that was because he'd been hurt, had seen his parents in a loveless relationship. But looking at him now, seeing that capacity to close himself off when she needed so very much for him to...let her in...

Last night was not the same for Rik, as for you. And whether or not he is like his father, you have to accept what he told you at the start. He won't ever love you, Mel. Not ever.

That attitude must make it much easier for Rik to deal with things like arranging this marriage and knowing he would be able to walk away from it later. It wasn't his fault that he'd asked her to help him. He had the right to try to protect his interests, and he'd wanted to help the people of Braston. His father had put him in an impossible position.

And now you have allowed yourself to end up in one, by falling for him.

All she could do was try to match his strength. She stared at the face she had come to cherish far too much in the short time she had known him, and prayed for that strength.

'Rik. I…' She didn't know what she wanted to say. What she should try to say.

'I was concerned. You may not be safe here, Melanie.'

If his frown showed anything but attention to her presence here at the fair, Mel couldn't discern it.

He went on. 'You are all on your own.'

Oh, she knew that more than well, though she realised that Rik meant it literally in this case.

A thousand moments of trying to escape wouldn't have got her any closer to feeling ready for this. For facing the feelings that had overcome her, and for facing him. She loved him. Deep down in her heart and soul, all those feelings had formed and intertwined and she had no choice about it.

How could Mel combat that? How could she take what had happened last night, and put it in some kind of perspective somehow so that she could contain these feelings, get them under control and then somehow make them stop altogether when it just wasn't like that now?

How could she marry him, live as his…princess but secretly in name only, let herself become more and more familiar with him with the passing of each day and then leave at the end of a few short months and get on with her life as though none of this had happened?

Those pretty, sparkly shoes were nowhere to be found right now.

'I came out to deliver some of the cakes that I baked last night for the festival.' Her words held a tremor and she cleared her throat before she went on. She didn't want that tremor. She couldn't allow it. She just couldn't. He mustn't detect how shaken she felt and perhaps figure out why.

Rik wanted a single life, not to be bound in the very relationship that he'd asked her to help him avoid. The knowledge lanced through her, of how utterly useless it would be to hold out any hope that their circumstances might change.

So press on, Mel. You can do it. One step after another until you get there.

'I wanted a look at the festival.' There. A normal tone, a normal topic of conversation.

A bunch of unspoken words filling the air between them.

She tightened her lips so they wouldn't tremble. 'I thought it might be interesting, and I didn't want the kitchen staff to have to bring all the cakes and cookies themselves.'

'And you had men lined up to ask you out.' His words held no particular inflection.

So why did Mel believe she could hear possession in them?

Because you are engaged to him, but for a purpose, Mel. That's all it is.

They might have been keeping their marriage plans secret from the masses for as long as they could possibly manage, but that wouldn't mean he would be happy to see her out being asked on dates by local men. 'I didn't expect that to happen. I just stepped out of the food tent.'

'I know. I saw.' Rik suppressed a sigh as he searched his fiancée's eyes, her face. She looked overwhelmed and uncertain, shaken to the core.

He blamed himself for that. And into that mix he had brought a burst of jealousy that was completely inappropriate.

'I should have waited for you this morning.' Whether he'd known what to say to her, or not, Rik should have waited. A prince did not avoid facing something just because he did not know how to manage a situation. 'Winnow called early and I went—'

'It's all right.' She touched his arm, and quickly drew her hand away as though the touch had burned her.

Remorse pricked him afresh. Remorse and a confusion of feelings? He pushed the impression aside. There were no warring feelings, just resolve and the need to try to ease them through this so they could go forward. Rik straightened his shoulders.

Melanie gestured in front of them. 'I've probably wasted your time, coming to look for me, too. Let's head back. I'm sure you have a lot of things that you need to do before the—the rehearsal later.'

'There is nothing that cannot wait until then.' But it was good that Melanie would come back with him now. For the first few minutes until they got free of the fair and started on the path back to the palace, Rik let silence reign.

Once they were alone, he slowed his pace. 'We need to talk, Melanie. About last night.'

'Oh, really, I don't think there's any need.' Every defence she could muster was immediately thrown up. She tipped her chin in the air. 'It's just—it was—we have our arrangement! Last night wasn't—it happened, that's all but it doesn't need to make any difference to anything. Nothing needs to change. Really I'd prefer to just forget all about it.'

'But that is not possible.' And even though he knew it should not have happened, Rik did not want...to deny the memory or to let her think— 'I don't want you to imagine that I took what we shared lightly,' he began carefully. 'It was—'

'Lots of people sleep together for lots of different reasons.' She drew a shuddery breath. 'We did because we did. We were...a little bit attracted to each other and maybe we were...curious. Now that curiosity is set to rest it doesn't have to happen again.' Her words emerged in stilted tones but with so much determination.

She was saying all the things that Rik himself believed about their situation. Not dismissing what they had shared, but doing all she could to put it in an appropriate context. This was what he would have tried to do himself, so why did her response make his chest feel tight? Make him want to take her in his arms again and try to mend them through touch when touch had brought them to this in the first place?

They rounded a bend in the road. The palace came into view.

Rik barely looked ahead of them. He could only look at Melanie. Guilt that he had caused her this unease vied with feelings of…disappointment and…loss within him. How could that be so? He must only feel relief, and…the need to reassure her.

So get your focus back on the goal, Rik. It's as important now as it was at the start.

It was. In her way, Melanie was right. Nothing about any of that had changed. Nothing at the core of him, either. Nothing of what he needed, of what he could give and…what he could not give.

So do what you can to reassure her, Rik, both for now and for later.

'I will look after you for the short term of our marriage, Melanie.' A rustle sounded around a bend in the path and he briefly wondered if Rufusina had got loose again before the thought left him for more important ones. 'You will lack for nothing. I will provide everything you might want, and when you go back to Australia afterwards—'

'I don't need anything extra from you. I still have all the money you gave me while we were in Paris. That's more than enough to see me back to Australia.' Her words were protective, proud. 'I can take care of myself once I've finished being your temporary princess. All that matters is that you've held onto your freedom, and you've got the things you needed—'

'What is this? What is going on here?' King Georgio appeared before them on the path.

Not Rufusina on the loose and foraging.

But Rik's father, becoming angrier by the moment as what he had just heard sank in.

'What trickery have I just heard, Rikardo? I did not say that you could marry temporarily. You must marry permanently!' His gaze shifted to Melanie and further suspicion filled it.

Before the king could speak, Rik took a step forward, half shielding Melanie with his body. 'This situation is of my making, Father. You will not question Melanie or accuse her about any of this.'

'Then you will explain yourself.' Georgio's words were cold. 'And this will not be done standing in the middle of a walkway.'

Security people had gathered in the king's wake.

'You will attend me appropriately, inside the palace. You will not keep me waiting.' Without another word, the older man walked away.

Rik turned to Melanie.

'All your plans, Rik.' Concern and unease filled her face. 'He looked so angry.'

'I must speak to him now, try to get him to understand.' He hesitated. 'You will wait for me?'

'I'll wait in our—in the suite until you can let me know what happened.'

With thoughts churning, Rik took one last look at the woman before him, and turned to follow his father.

CHAPTER TWELVE

I AM stunned.

Rik thought the words silently as he walked towards the grand historic church where he and Melanie were to today rehearse the marriage ceremony. Stunned almost to the point of numbness by what his father had just revealed.

He needed to speak to Melanie now more than before, and when he stepped through the doors of the church, she broke away from the small group of people gathered near the front of the large ancient building, and rushed to his side.

'I couldn't wait for you any longer.' She said the words in a hushed whisper. 'Dominico came to get me and I couldn't tell him anything was wrong. Is—is the wedding off now? What happened? What did your father say?'

Beyond them, Anrai and Marcelo waited, along with the priest and various others expecting to participate in this marriage ceremony next week.

Another brother could be standing there.

'This will shock you, as it did me when my father revealed it, and I would ask that you not tell anyone until I can speak to Anrai and Marcelo.' Rik drew a slow breath. 'The reason that my father pushed so hard for marriages is because there is an older brother, a love child to a woman in England. Two years ago this man discovered his true identity. He's been trying to gain a position in the family through my father since.'

'Is—? That isn't sounding like good news to you?' Melanie's hand half lifted as though she would press it over her mouth before she dropped it away again.

'His existence is the reason my mother left, and he has now gained access to copies of our family law and worked out that he can try to claim ascendancy and, with it, Marcelo's position, rights, and work. If Marcelo is married, his position is safe, but until we are also married, Anrai's and mine...are not.'

'In other words he doesn't really belong within the family.' She said it quietly. 'He's not wanted.'

'He is not royal born.' Rik said it carefully. 'Whether he will find a place within the family, at this stage I do not know. I would like to meet him and discern for myself what manner of man he is and go from there. I would not reject a brother, but I also would not welcome a threat to the security of my country and people.'

'That's fair.' She seemed to relax as she said the words.

Rik went on. 'The old laws—this is part of why Marcelo wants to bring change. This is not merely so we can all maintain our positions. It is to keep the people of the country safe as well.'

'Why would this man push for a position that

shouldn't rightly be his? Surely he must realise that he can't just walk in and take someone's place?'

'My father has no doubt contributed to the man's anger and frustration by refusing to acknowledge him at all when he should have done so many years ago.'

'Well, you can take care of your part in it. You're marrying me. You can say you've been married then. Your position will be safe!'

All but for one vital thing. 'I must *remain married*, Melanie. My plan to marry you and then end the relationship afterwards will not work for this.'

'What—what will you do?' She searched his face and her eyes were so deep and so guarded as she began to realise how this new situation had raised the stakes. 'You'll need to find someone else. You'll need to start looking right away. Someone you can make that kind of commitment with. There must be *someone* you could accept in that way.'

The priest cleared his throat noisily at the front of the church.

Rik's brothers cast glances their way that were becoming more than curious.

Of all settings and times, this had to be about the worst but at least as Rik had informed Melanie of the basics of the issue his thoughts had cleared. He knew exactly what he needed, now, and from whom, but could he yet again convince her?

'You want me to be the one, don't you?' The words came from between lips that had whitened with shock. 'You want me to be married to you permanently?'

'We are already together. I would provide for your

every need. You would live a privileged life, want for nothing.' It would resolve problems, not only for Rik, but also for Melanie. 'You would never again have to fend for yourself, and later if you wanted a child I would…allow it.'

There were other words that tried to bubble up, but Rik needed to protect himself in this—

Her glance searched his face before it shifted to take in the church, the people waiting for the rehearsal to start. 'I can't do it. Not even for the people.' She whispered the words before she added more strongly, 'I've tried hard in my life and I've never rejected people even when they've rejected me, but I won't line up for another lifetime of that.

'I blamed myself for losing my parents in that car crash. I thought after that I didn't deserve happiness, to be alive when they weren't, but that was grief talking. I do deserve happiness. I deserve better from you.'

Melanie turned on her heel and ran from the church.

CHAPTER THIRTEEN

'I'VE made the biggest mistake of my life.' Rik spoke the words to Marcelo as his brother drove them towards the country's small international airport. He felt sick inside, close to overwhelmed and very, very afraid that he might have lost his chance with Melanie for ever by stupidly trying too hard to protect himself and by being too slow to realise…

Rik had lost valuable time searching for Melanie out of doors. He'd thought she must have run to their spot on the mountainside, or perhaps back to Ettonbierre village to lose herself in the crowd there.

As he'd searched, knowing his brothers were also looking, Rik had begun to panic. In her distraught state, what if something happened to Melanie? And all that he had locked down inside him and tried to deny since he and Melanie made love had begun to inexorably make its way to the surface and demand to be known.

'She will not leave the airport.' Marcelo offered the assurance without taking his glance from the road. 'If need be, the flights will all be delayed until we get there. Dominico will take care of it.'

That was a privilege of position that, in this moment, Rik was willing to exploit without compunction. It was Melanie's reaction when he caught up with her that concerned him.

'I have used Melanie without considering how she might feel. Not respected her rights and emotions.' He shook his head. 'I asked her to remain permanently married to me as though she should be grateful for all the privileges she would receive as part of the family.'

'Such as being in a loveless marriage for life?' Marcelo's words were not harsh, neither teasing, but a statement of understanding of things that he and Rik had never discussed about their upbringing.

'I wanted to avoid that at all costs.' Why hadn't Rik understood sooner that his drive to pull Melanie into exactly that long-term relationship had not been fuelled merely by the need to protect his position and that of his brothers, in the knowledge of this unknown brother? It had been driven by need of *Melanie*. And yet he felt no warmth towards this unknown man. 'I cannot find soft emotion in my heart for him, Marcelo. Even now when I realise how I feel about Melanie—'

'One thing at a time,' Marcelo advised. He drew the car to a halt in a no stopping zone in front of the airport. 'We all need to get to know this man. Good luck, brother.'

Rik met Marcelo's gaze as he threw the car door open. 'Thank you.'

Rik drew a deep breath and strode quickly into the airport terminal.

* * *

I'm not going to feel guilty about the money.

Melanie thought this as she twisted her hands together in her lap. She'd packed all her luggage, half dreading that Rik might appear at any moment. Then she'd summoned palace staff to carry it all downstairs and put it in the cab she'd ordered. A real cab this time, with no mix-ups.

She'd bought an airline ticket to get back to Australia. The flight wasn't going directly there. She'd asked for the first one that would get her out of the country and she'd used the money Rik had given her that day in Paris, to pay for it.

It was almost time, just a few more minutes and she would be able to board the plane, and…fly away from Braston, and from Rik, for ever.

Her heart squeezed and she forced her gaze forward. Other people in the boarding lounge talked to each other or relaxed in their chairs, at ease with themselves and their plans. Mel just wanted to…get through this. She felt she was letting down the people, but Rik would find someone else. Prince Rikardo Eduard Ettonbierre of Braston would not struggle to find a woman willing to marry him for life.

Mel couldn't be that woman. Not without love.

'Melanie!'

At first she thought she'd imagined his familiar voice, a figment within her mind because her heart hurt so much. It was going to take time to get past those raw emotions and begin to heal.

Could she heal from falling in love with Rik?

'Mel. Thank goodness you're here.' Rik appeared

in front of her. Ruffled. Surprisingly un-prince-like with his tie askew and his suit coat hanging open. *Real.*

Mel shot to her feet. She wasn't sure what she intended to do when she got upright. Run? Faint? Throw herself at him and hope against hope that he would open his arms and his heart to her?

Get real, Melanie Watson. You're still a cook and he's still a prince and he doesn't love you and that's that.

'I don't have a glass slipper.' His words were low.

And confusing. 'I—I don't understand.'

Words came over the airport speaker system. French and then English. Her flight was being called. Mel had to get on the flight. She glanced towards the gate, to people beginning to go through. Her heart said stay. Her survival instincts said go. Go and don't look back because you've done that "love people and not be loved in return" thing and it just hurts too damned much to do it again. 'I have to go, Rik. I paid all your money to buy the ticket. I can't buy another one.'

'I will buy you another ticket, Mel.' He lifted his hand as though he would take hers, and hesitated as though uncertain of his welcome. 'If you still want to go.'

Oh, Rik.

'Please. I left out something very important when I asked you to marry me.'

'Another bargaining chip?' She hadn't meant to say it. She didn't want to spread hurt, or reveal her heart. Mel just wanted…to go home and yet, where was home now? Could home be anywhere when her heart had already decided where it wanted to be? 'I didn't mean that.'

'You had every right to say it.' Rik gestured to a room to their left. 'There's a private lounge there. Will you give me a few minutes, Mel? Please? You will still be able to make this flight if you want to, or a next one. Anything you want, but please let me try—'

'All right.' She led the way to the room, pushed the door open and stepped inside. Somehow it felt important to take that initiative. To be in charge even if she was agreeing to stall her plans to speak with him.

It was a small room. The lounge suite was quintessential airport "luxury". Deep red velvet with large cushions all immaculately kept. There were matching drapes opened wide and a view of runways with planes in various stages of arrival and departure.

All Mel could see was Rik's blue eyes, fixed on her brown ones, searching as though there was something that he desperately needed to find.

'This isn't a fairy tale, Rik. I know you're a prince but to me you'll always be a man first. You'll be Rik, who I—' Fell in love with. She bit back the words.

'No. There is little of the fairy tale about current circumstances and I confess I was shocked by my father's announcement of a secret brother.' Rik did take her hand now, and led her to a lounge seat.

Somehow they were seated with her hand still held in his and far too much of a feeling of rightness inside Mel's foolish, foolish heart. 'I hope that situation can be worked out so that nobody loses too much.'

'I do not know what is possible. I have not had time

to get all the facts together, let alone think of how to act on any of them.' For this moment Rik brushed the topic aside. 'Melanie, I asked you to marry me permanently—'

'But deep down even though you have to do it, you don't want to be tied in a relationship like that, and I... can't do it when—' She ground to a halt.

'When I offered all those things that don't matter to you, and nothing else? They never have.' One side of Rik's mouth lifted in a wry, self-mocking twist. 'Everything that makes me a prince, that might appeal, doesn't matter to you. I was too slow to think about that, and too slow to understand why I needed so much for you to agree to help me anyway.'

Was it care that she saw in his eyes? Mel didn't want to hope. Not now. Not when she'd made up her mind to go and that was the only solution. 'You'll find someone, Rik. You'll be able to marry and hold onto your job. I'm sorry it will have to be for all your life. I'm sorry for that.'

Each word tightened the ache in her chest. Each glance at him made it harder to keep the tremor out of her voice.

'The thing is, all that has changed for me, Melanie. It has changed because I fell in love with you.' His words were low. Raw.

Real? Mel frowned. Shook her head. There was no allergy medication to blame now. Nothing but a hope and sense of loss so deep that she was afraid she'd heard those words only inside her, afraid to hear them at all, and so she denied. 'No.'

'The moment I took you into my arms and made love to you, I fell in love with you.' This time when he said it, emotion crowded *his* face. 'Please believe me that this is true.'

Mel had never seen that emotion, except…lurking in the backs of his eyes when he held her last night…

Could she believe this? Could Rik truly have fallen in love with her? 'You're a prince.'

'As you said when we first met.' He inclined his head. His eyes didn't twinkle, but memory was there.

'I'm a cook. From Australia.' A commoner with no fixed abode. 'I didn't even know how to curtsy properly.'

Do you really love me, Rik?

Could he really love *her*, Nicole Melanie Watson? 'You said you would never love.'

'I didn't know there would be you, and that you would come to live, not only at the palace, but that you would move into my heart.' He took both her hands into his.

She glanced down. 'The ring! I meant to leave it in the suite.'

'*Our* suite. I am glad you didn't take it off.' He touched the diamonds. 'It is made to be there.' His gaze lifted to hers. 'I know I am asking for another leap of faith, and if you cannot find anything in your heart for me then I will accept it, but I am hoping against all hope that you will agree to give me a chance to show you how deeply I have come to love you.'

'I want to, Rik.' Oh, she wanted to do that with all of *her* heart. 'If you truly love me—'

'I do.' He didn't hesitate. Conviction filled his tone. 'If you can learn to love *me*, I will be the happiest man in the world.'

'That was what you meant about the glass slipper.' She hadn't realised that he wanted to make her his princess truly, in every way. 'I'm a practical girl, Rik. I like cooking and I lost my parents and grew up trying to be loved and my aunt and uncle and Nicolette didn't, and I promised myself I would never be hurt like that again.'

But she'd opened her heart to Rik and he...loved her. 'Are you sure? Because I don't know how you could have overcome all that. You were so firmly fixed that you wouldn't be able to have that kind of relationship.'

'I thought I was incapable of experiencing those feelings. Love, commitment.'

'Your upbringing harmed you.' Mel didn't want to hurt him with the words, but they were part of *his* history, of who he was.

'We have both experienced hurt at the hands of family.' There was regret and acknowledgement, and love shining in his eyes openly for her now. 'But you have set all of my love free.'

Mel believed it then. She let go of the last doubt and took her leap of faith. 'I fell in love with you, too, Rik. I thought I was going to help you to solve a problem and then go back to Australia. Instead I wanted to stay with you for ever, but when you asked me—'

'I stupidly didn't realise what those feelings inside meant.' He drew a breath that wasn't quite steady. 'I thought I'd lost you. I couldn't bear that thought.' Again his fingers touched her ring as he drew her to her feet with him and held both her hands. 'Will you marry me next week, Mel? Give me a chance to show you every day for ever how much you mean to me?'

'Yes.' Melanie said it and stepped into his arms and, oh, it felt right. So, so right, to be in Rik's arms, in the prince's arms, where she belonged. There were no sparkly shoes. She wasn't down a rabbit hole. She had simply…come home to this man of her dreams. 'Yes, I will marry you next week and stay married for ever, and love you every single day while you love me every single day.'

Mel knew there would be hurdles. She was marrying a prince! But she would give all of her heart to him and now she knew that she could trust it into his love and care.

He glanced out of the window and smiled. 'You've missed your flight. Let's go…home and start counting the days until next week.'

'The wedding planner is going to be relieved that she doesn't have to start all over again.' A smile started on Melanie's face and she tucked her arm through Rik's and they left the room and made their way out of the airport to a car parked and waiting for Rik. The keys were in it, just as though it had been brought for him and left specially.

Well, it would have been, wouldn't it? Mel thought. After all, he was a prince.

And Melanie Watson, cook, was marrying him.

For now and for ever.

And that seemed exactly right.

EPILOGUE

'THERE is nothing to be nervous about.' Anrai spoke the words to Melanie as they made their way towards the rear-entry door of the church. 'And thank you for allowing me to be the one to escort you for this occasion.'

Melanie drew a deep breath and glanced at her soon-to-be brother-in-law from beneath the filmy bridal veil. Excitement filled her. This was the moment that she and Rik had worked towards, and that now would be the fulfilment of very new and special dreams for them. 'You know that I love him.'

'Yes. He is lucky. I do not profess to hold similar hope for myself, but I am glad that you have found each other.' Anrai's words were warm, accepting, and then the doors were thrown open and music started and they began the long walk to the front of the church.

Soft gasps filled the air as guests saw the beautiful gown, the train that whispered behind her. A hint of lace. Tiny pearls stitched in layers. A princess neckline for an everyday girl about to become that princess.

Mel's glance shifted to one row of seats in the church. To her uncle, and aunt, and her cousin. Her gaze meshed with Nicolette's for a moment. Nicolette looked attractive in a pale pink chiffon gown. But today the attention was all for Melanie.

For a moment Mel felt a prick of sadness, but she couldn't make her cousin see that love came from within, was a gift so much more important than any material thing.

It was Nicolette who looked away, who couldn't seem to hold her cousin's gaze any longer.

And then there was Rik at the front of the church, waiting faithfully without glancing back until Anrai arrived with Mel on his arm and passed her hand to Rik's arm, placing it there as Mel's father would have done if he'd been here.

Warmth spread through Mel's chest as she looked into her prince's eyes and saw the love and happiness there and somehow she thought her parents might have been watching. She felt their love and warmth, too.

'Dearly beloved…' The priest began the service.

And there before God and his witnesses, Nicole Melanie Watson married Rikardo Eduard Ettonbierre, third prince of Braston.

He *did* have several titles and various bits of land.

His wife-to-be *was* a wonderful cook.

And they were still working on the agreement about who got ownership of any of Rufusina's offspring should the hog ever choose to bless them with a litter.

But Rik and Mel were happy today, and they would remain happy. And Rufusina's offspring were a whole other legend…

* * * * *

COMING NEXT MONTH from Harlequin® Romance

#4327 NANNY FOR THE MILLIONAIRE'S TWINS
First Time Dads!
Susan Meier
Chance Montgomery lays the past to rest with the help of his adorable twin babies and their beautiful nanny, Tory.

#4328 SLOW DANCE WITH THE SHERIFF
The Larkville Legacy
Nikki Logan
Ex-ballerina Ellie leaves Manhattan behind to look for answers in sleepy Larkville, but instead finds dreamy county sheriff, Jed Jackson....

#4329 THE NAVY SEAL'S BRIDE
Heroes Come Home
Soraya Lane
Navy SEAL Tom is struggling with civilian life. Can beautiful teacher Caitlin crack the walls around this soldier's battle-worn heart?

#4330 ALWAYS THE BEST MAN
Fiona Harper
Before their best friends' wedding is over, will ice-cool Damien realize he's the best man for bubbly bridesmaid Zoe?

#4331 HOW THE PLAYBOY GOT SERIOUS
The McKenna Brothers
Shirley Jump
Playboy Riley discovers that it will take more than his blue eyes and easy smile to impress feisty waitress Stace....

#4332 NEW YORK'S FINEST REBEL
Trish Wylie
Sparks fly when fashionista Jo realizes her sworn enemy—the infuriatingly attractive cop, Daniel Brannigan—has moved in next door!

You can find more information on upcoming Harlequin® titles, free excerpts and more at www.Harlequin.com.

HRCNM0712

REQUEST YOUR FREE BOOKS!
2 FREE NOVELS PLUS 2 FREE GIFTS!

Harlequin *Romance*

From the Heart, For the Heart

YES! Please send me 2 FREE Harlequin® Romance novels and my 2 FREE gifts (gifts are worth about $10). After receiving them, if I don't wish to receive any more books, I can return the shipping statement marked "cancel". If I don't cancel, I will receive 6 brand-new novels every month and be billed just $4.09 per book in the U.S. or $4.49 per book in Canada. That's a savings of at least 14% off the cover price! It's quite a bargain! Shipping and handling is just 50¢ per book in the U.S. and 75¢ per book in Canada.* I understand that accepting the 2 free books and gifts places me under no obligation to buy anything. I can always return a shipment and cancel at any time. Even if I never buy another book, the two free books and gifts are mine to keep forever.

116/316 HDN FESE

Name	(PLEASE PRINT)	
Address		Apt. #
City	State/Prov.	Zip/Postal Code

Signature (if under 18, a parent or guardian must sign)

Mail to the **Reader Service:**
IN U.S.A.: P.O. Box 1867, Buffalo, NY 14240-1867
IN CANADA: P.O. Box 609, Fort Erie, Ontario L2A 5X3

Not valid for current subscribers to Harlequin Romance books.

**Are you a subscriber to Harlequin Romance books
and want to receive the larger-print edition?
Call 1-800-873-8635 or visit www.ReaderService.com.**

* Terms and prices subject to change without notice. Prices do not include applicable taxes. Sales tax applicable in N.Y. Canadian residents will be charged applicable taxes. Offer not valid in Quebec. This offer is limited to one order per household. All orders subject to credit approval. Credit or debit balances in a customer's account(s) may be offset by any other outstanding balance owed by or to the customer. Please allow 4 to 6 weeks for delivery. Offer available while quantities last.

Your Privacy—The Reader Service is committed to protecting your privacy. Our Privacy Policy is available online at www.ReaderService.com or upon request from the Reader Service.

We make a portion of our mailing list available to reputable third parties that offer products we believe may interest you. If you prefer that we not exchange your name with third parties, or if you wish to clarify or modify your communication preferences, please visit us at www.ReaderService.com/consumerchoice or write to us at Reader Service Preference Service, P.O. Box 9062, Buffalo, NY 14269. Include your complete name and address.

HR11B

USA TODAY *bestselling author Lynne Graham brings you a brand-new story of passion and drama.*

THE SECRETS SHE CARRIED

"Don't play games with me," she urged, breathing in deeply and slowly, nostrils flaring in dismay at the familiar spicy scent of his designer aftershave.

The smell of him, so achingly familiar, unleashed a tide of memories. But Cristo had not made a commitment to her, had not done anything to make her feel secure and had never once mentioned love or the future. At the end of the day, in spite of all her precautions, he had still walked away untouched while she had been crushed in the process.

The knowledge that she had meant so little to him that he had ditched her to marry another woman still burned like acid inside her.

"Maybe I'm hoping you'll finally come clean," Cristo murmured levelly.

Erin turned her head, smooth brow indented with a frown as she struggled to recall the conversation and get back into it again. "Come clean about what?"

Cristo pulled off the road into a layby before he responded. "I found out what you were up to while you were working for me at the Mobila spa."

Erin twisted her entire body around to look at him, crystalline eyes flaring bright, her rising tension etched in the taut set of her heart-shaped face. "What do you mean... what I was up to?"

Cristo looked at her levelly, ebony dark eyes cool and opaque as frosted glass. "You were stealing from me."

"I am not a thief," Erin repeated doggedly, although an alarm bell had gone off in her head the instant he mentioned the theft and sale of products from the store.

"I have the proof," Cristo retorted crisply. "You can't talk or charm your way out of this, Erin—"

"I'm not interested in charming you. I'm not the same woman I was when we were together," Erin countered curtly, for what he had done to her had toughened her. There was nothing like surviving an unhappy love affair to build self-knowledge and character, she reckoned painfully. He had broken her heart, taught her how fragile she was, left her bitter and humiliated. But she had had to pick herself up again fast once she'd discovered that she was pregnant.

Cristo is going to make Erin pay back
what he believes she stole—in whatever way he
demands.... But little does he know that Erin's about
to drop two very important bombshells!

**Pick up a copy of *THE SECRETS SHE CARRIED*
by Lynne Graham, available August 2012
from Harlequin Presents®.**

Harlequin® Super Romance®

*Enjoy a month of compelling, emotional stories, including
a poignant new tale of love lost and found from*

Sarah Mayberry

When Angela Bartlett loses her best friend to a rare heart
condition, it seems only natural that she step in and help
widower and friend Michael Young. The last thing she
expects is to find herself falling for him....

Within Reach

Available August 7!

> "I loved it. I thought the story was very believable.
> The characters were endearing. The author wrote beautifully...
> I will be looking for future books by Sarah Mayberry."
>
> —Sherry, Harlequin® Superromance® reader, on *Her Best Friend*

Find more great stories this month from
Harlequin® Superromance® at

www.Harlequin.com

HSRSM71795